Octave Thanet

An Adventure in Photography

Octave Thanet

An Adventure in Photography

ISBN/EAN: 9783742819925

Manufactured in Europe, USA, Canada, Australia, Japa

Cover: Foto ©Andreas Hilbeck / pixelio.de

Manufactured and distributed by brebook publishing software
(www.brebook.com)

Octave Thanet

An Adventure in Photography

✹ ✹ ✹ AN ADVENTURE IN
PHOTOGRAPHY ✹ ✹ ✹
✹ ✹ BY OCTAVE THANET
ILLUSTRATED FROM PHOTOGRAPHS
BY THE ADVENTURERS ✹ ✹

✹ CHARLES SCRIBNER'S SONS
NEW YORK 1893 ✹ ✹ ✹

Press of J. J. Little & Co.
Astor Place, New York

CONTENTS

CHAPTER I

Contents

LIST OF ILLUSTRATIONS

List of Illustrations

x

List of Illustrations

xi

THE BLACK RIVER.

(Taken with a $10 Waterbury lens.)

AN

ADVENTURE IN PHOTOGRAPHY

CHAPTER I

SHOWING HOW WE MEANT WELL

WHEN my kind friends, the publishers, first proposed this book to me, I at once laid the proposition before my partner.

Jane and I have taken photographs, developed photographs, printed and mounted photographs, together, for four years.

"But we don't know enough to write a book," said Jane.

"And they want us to illustrate it with our own photographs," I continued, under the impetus of my first burst of information, although I felt a distinct shock, similar to the feeling produced by unexpected cold water.

"But we don't make good enough photographs to illustrate a book," said Jane.

I did not discuss the question of fact; Jane has a

1

great deal on her side of the argument, as the ash-barrel and I know better than any one; I retreated in good order and made a flank movement.

"We have failed in so many different and unexpected ways," I urged, "I think it would be interesting and—and profitable to amateur photographers to read about them : I know *we* should have been very grateful to get a book that did not say a word about the scientific action of the developer, or have all the higher mathematics in tow about the exposures and the shutter."

"Well, maybe," Jane admitted; "but I don't want to pretend to be photographic swells when all we can do is to make passable pictures."

Therefore this little book makes no pretension to authority, neither can it claim any original discoveries; it is simply the record of the failures and good fortunes of two amateurs, forced by circumstances to depend considerably upon their own ingenuity; and shows what may be done by any amateur student, without a very large expenditure of money or of time.

If nothing else shall be accomplished, the author fondly hopes that it will reveal the moral possibilities of photography as the Educator, I may say the Compeller, of the sterner and simpler virtues that a luxurious *fin de siècle* discourages. The photographer—especially the amateur, for the professional photographer has con-

veniences—must be a stoic, not heeding cold, heat,
mosquitoes, strange dogs sniffing a sinister sniff at his
heels, or cows playfully charging down the middle distance with lowered horns, or gurgling and flaring and
bursting red lanterns, or peril, or exasperation, or despair. He must be orderly and exact. He must have
exceeding patience and a good deal of muscle. He
must be slow of faith, following the advice of the apostle
and "trying all things;" but holding fast to a very
few. I don't say that he should be modest, because
modesty is a virtue likely to force herself upon him
whether he wills or no, particularly if he attempt to
join a camera club.

When I consider the further benefit of the art-science
to the character, by its action as a spiritual re-agent,
detecting faults of temper and habit of which the pos-
sessor, but for this bitter but salutary enlightenment,
might never be aware, it almost seems to me that it
ought to be taught in all the theological schools, as a
sort of moral annex.

Our own introduction to photography was quite
unpremeditated. My friend's mother and I gave Jane
a camera for a present. We read some especially glow-
ing advertisements, and we were captured. At this time
we were spending the winter on an Arkansas plantation,
owned jointly by my friends and a gentleman of Arkansas who manages the plantation. The planter was going

3

to St. Louis to buy goods for the plantation store; he agreed to buy a camera at the same time. He returned with a Rochester Optical Company's Model Camera, with all the accompaniments thereof, and a quantity of miscellaneous information obtained from an obliging young man who sold the camera. The lens was a Waterbury lens, and the illustrations of this chapter are all taken by this lens, during our first winter at the camera. The year following, we bought a handsome fifty-dollar camera and a fifty-dollar lens, an Orthographic lens a size larger than the camera, to counteract distortion. The first camera only cost twenty-six dollars. With it, included in the price, was the usual photographic outfit of humble life: a dozen five-by-eight plates, a dozen half plates, a developing tray, a printing tray, a washing tray, a fixing tray, a slide holder, a printing frame, a bottle of developer, a bottle of toning fluid, some hyposulphite of soda for fixing, a package of blue paper, and a package of that albumen-coated paper which our English cousins call preserved paper.

"Where are we going to have a studio?" one of us ventured to ask; "don't we need some place to do the pictures in, Madonna?"

"Oh, no," said Jane, cheerfully. There was a little book in the outfit. There is always a little book inclosed in these outfits, by some thoughtful manufacturer of photographic implements. It is devoted to the encouragement of the amateur and the glorification of the special brand of goods of the aforesaid missionary manufacturer. Jane knew our little book by heart. She had mastered all its platitudes about how grateful we ought to feel for our five senses, how beautiful is nature, and how careful we must be about getting hyposulphite of soda into anything.

"Oh, no," says Jane, brimming over with little book lore; "it says" (she always spoke of the little book as It, just as some women always speak of their husbands as He!) "it says any dark closet will do, or, if you don't have a dark closet, any room at night. It says the kitchen is very convenient, because of the running water and the pans."

"But aren't your mixtures poisonous?" says Madonna, a little dubiously.

"Deadly," comes from the other member of the firm. "Your little book is an out-and-out assassin!"

Nevertheless, how many poisons have gone down our kitchen sink I shudder to compute. Jane said they went down into the drain, and that it was only once in a while we left what the doctors call a lethal draught, standing about, and that she was very particular whenever she used the kitchen spoons to stir our oxalate of potash (a very little of which taken into the human system goes a great way, I am informed) to cleanse them thoroughly afterwards, and she always covered the oxalate in heating it on the stove, in order that it might not spatter into the viands preparing on the stove at the same time; and she never left it alone lest Jinny (our black cook) should taste it by mistake. She did not, she said darkly, know what *I* might have done!

Jinny was not poisoned, and the dog and cat escaped, but I was not surprised that our fowls should, like Lady Clara Vere de Vere, "sicken with a vague disease," for I had seen them pecking (with the fatal inquisitiveness of the hen) at our poisons as they oozed from the drain.

It was later, I think, that we discovered a fact in zoology, or rather entomology, namely, the marvellous tenacity of life in the common house fly. Two grains of pyrogallic acid will kill a dog; but flies simply dote on it, either as a beverage or as a medicinal powder sprinkled on meat. They return again and again to the feast with fresh zest. We never by any chance could find a dead fly in our studio. Mosquitoes, gnats, and such small banditti did occasionally drown in the developer or the hypo bath; but the wary fly sipped and flew away rejoicing, singing as he flew, and we were reduced to stick up a sheet of the inhuman sticky fly paper to help our screens.

We began without a studio. We spent days in focussing. That is what the little book advised. So we

—

used to go out with the camera and spend an hour at a time, staring at nothing in particular, and trying to see it clearly, like a novelist of the most advanced realist school.

I was away when the first picture was taken. Jane and the planter took it with every possible care; Jane holding the little book, the planter removing the slide slowly and cautiously, and taking off the cap, while Jane counted. The picture was developed and printed, and waiting to welcome me.

Madonna displayed it with maternal pride. "Jenny developed and printed it all herself," she said.

It was a large, pale house on a little shelf of foreground, against a small, dark sky. I couldn't think that it was pretty; but it plainly was a house, and Jane had done it all herself. I was impressed.

It was printed on blue paper, very blue paper; the high lights were light blue, and the shadows were dark blue. The blue paper came with the outfit.

"What makes the sky and the trees the same color?" said Madonna, eying it tenderly; "is that the paper? They are not, in the photographs you buy."

"It is because it is a thin negative," said Jane.

"What's the difference between a thin negative and a fat one?" said I.

"You mean a dense negative; dense and thin is what they call them," corrected Jane; "a thin negative is one

7

that has been exposed too long when the picture was taken. The book says that even professional photographers sometimes mistake the proper time for an exposure; but that in a little while, if you are careful, you can guess near enough. It is very important to expose long enough, because, if you don't, the details will not come out at all; but you must not expose too long, because then the details will come, but there will be no contrast."

"It seems to be difficult," I ventured feebly.

We thought so more and more, as the days rolled by and our stock of plates diminished. There are so many things to remember in taking a picture; sometimes one forgets to remove the slide, and sometimes the cap, and sometimes we took pictures without the stops, although much more often we used the wrong stops. The light has a sneaking way of getting into the plate-holder through cracks, or into the bellows of the camera; while dust is as insidious as sin. Once the focusing-cloth slipped over the lens and threw a pall over a cotton picking. After we secured a plate on which was a presumable picture, there were all the perils of development. Either the picture came up in a flash, with the sky and the foliage of the same tint of ash, or it was all black and white, with no detail in the shadow, or—a frequent tragedy—it did not come at all!

Out of the first box of plates we secured two nega-

" ONCE THE FOCUSING CLOTH SLIPPED. "

tives from which it was possible to print. And the second box did not encourage us much more. I recall the first time we developed, because I think we made about as many mistakes as the amateur can make, even with the aid of a little book.

We used a corner of the dining-room for a dark room, and we waited for a moonless night, which was an inconvenience, because, having but one plate-holder, we could take no more pictures until the first taken were safely out of the plate-holder. We had not then discovered that a plate with a picture on it is as safe as a plate without one, in the common plate-box of commerce. Later we took dozens of pictures, taking our day's work out of the slides at night and shifting it into a plate-box, covering with black paper and wrapping the box up in black cloth, and when the box was full pasting it securely. But at this period we had no empty plate-boxes; besides, we no more dared to take liberties with those mysterious pictures than to taste our drugs. The little book told us to take a dark night, and we took it. We took also three trays, a jug of water, and an empty water-bucket to the table. Then Jane suggested that we have a second bucket, full of water, so as to be sure to have enough water.

"The book says, 'Wash well,' and put in a rack to dry," said Jane, musingly; "it only says 'rinse' after developing, 'rinse and place in the fixing solution.'

9

What do you suppose 'wash well' means? To wash off two or three times?"

I thought it did mean that; and we took the bucket of water. We poured a narrow stream several times over the plate, and we told each other that whatever might be wrong with the development in other respects, at least we were washing the plates thoroughly. It chilled us to read, later, that half an hour's washing with running water ought "to eliminate the hypo."

"Why, it must take gallons on gallons of water!" cried Jane, "and running water, too; it will not do, they all say, to simply let the negatives soak."

"We might pump it at the kitchen sink," suggested Madonna. "Jim could pump for you, or, if you don't want to risk his pumping, I would as lief pump as not."

It ended in our buying a negative-box of zinc—a box large enough to hold a dozen negatives—and pumping into it for half an hour. Then our minds simultaneously (so simultaneously that I suspect we must have read it somewhere) evolved the scheme of fitting a faucet-cock to a kerosene barrel, placing the negative-box beneath, turning the cock partially, and letting the water of the whole hogshead drip down on the negatives and drain off into space. "So much has been said, and on the whole so well said," about the water entering a negative-box from below, and rising, like honest industry, with a pause for remarks at every stage, until

10

---

it flows over the top, that we were impressed, and bought a rubber tube and fitted it on to the cock at one end and to a little funnel inserted into the box at the other. The box is Anthony's Washing-box, and any one who uses it can easily make the same arrangement. It looked so neat and comfortable, and was so in accord with the principles of science, that it pains me to have to mention that one end usually slipped off while we were gone, and the water careered aimlessly about the back yard, leaving the negatives stranded high and dry. Therefore, reluctantly, we abandoned the scientific method, and let our water drip in and flow out according to the laws of gravitation, which seem to work pretty steadily, even on a Southern plantation.

Our custom is to put the negatives to soak for an hour, then to wash them off well and go over the surface with a little piece ("a dab" is Jane's definition of size) of absorbent cotton. This takes away a disagreeable streaky effect that may disturb an otherwise blameless negative, as a poor digestion will the disposition of a saint.

Our first negatives had no such advantages, you may be sure; they were washed but not cleansed. They ought by all the chances to have come to the worst kind of grief; but they were as obstinate as the sinners who live to ninety in spite of their whiskey and tobacco; we printed from them for years; they were thin, they were flat, they took to every kind of dissipation in silver stains; but they did not fade, neither did they spot, in fine, they acted as if they were perfectly washed. Their conduct caused one of us disquieting doubts. Can it be, whispered a cynical suspicion, that hypo is less a villain than he is painted; that it is more important to thoroughly fix your image than it is to wash off the fixing?

But to return to our first efforts. We took the plates into our improvised studio in the dining-room, where we artlessly protected the matting on the floor, with newspapers. We lit our lantern. It was about the size of a fist, and of the type known among photographers as the Oculist's Friend. It illumined a circle on the plate rather bigger than a dollar. The other parts of the table were in Cimmerian darkness. The position of the graduate—we had but one—the bottles that took the place of graduates, the chemicals and the trays, all must be learned by heart before the séance began, for fear of accidents—which generally occurred anyhow!

Jane sat in the operating chair. She had fortified herself for the occasion beforehand by reading the little book. I stood in waiting. It was very dark. The plate-holder was in Jane's hand. Plate-holders are of all sorts and descriptions. One thing which the amateur does not always consider, in buying plates, he is like to have to consider so soon as he shall unload them, namely the contrivance by which the plate is held in place with-

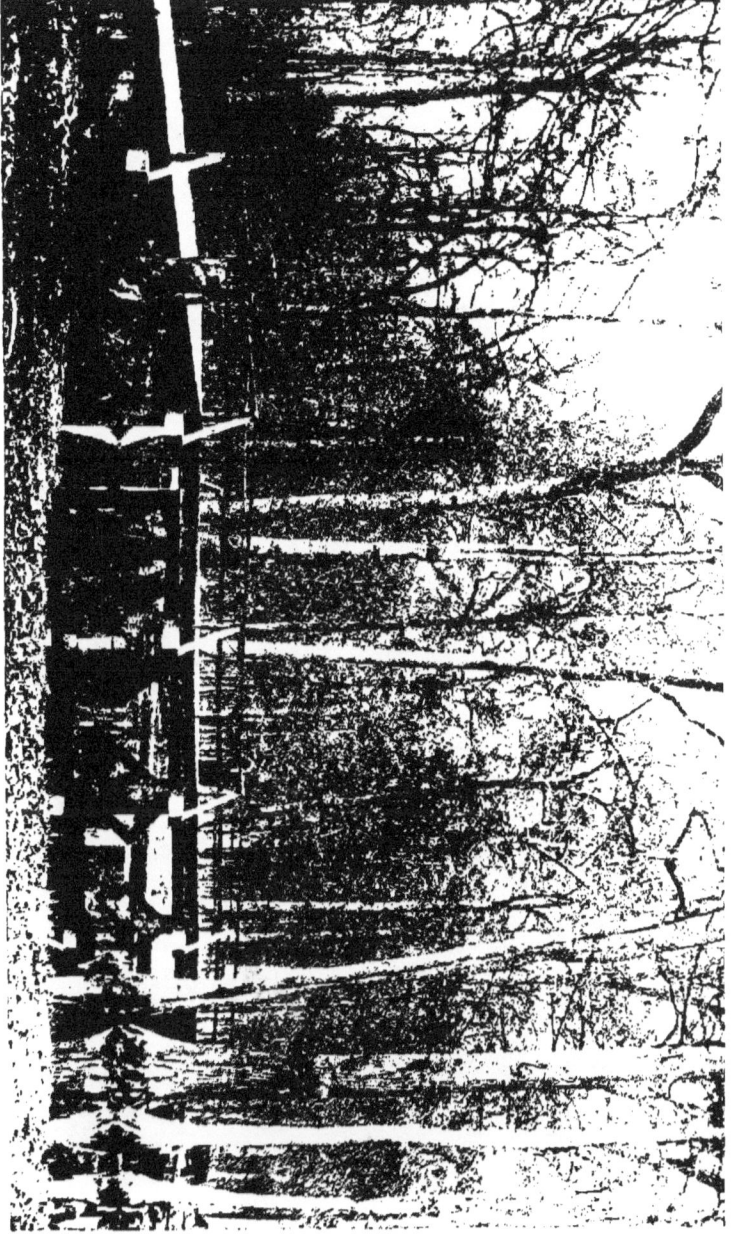

RUNNING WATER.

(Waterbury lens.)

in the holder. Our first plate-holders had a kind of
screw attachment which, the advertisements said, " held
the plates immovable." For once the advertisements
were quite truthful, immovable is precisely the word for
the grip of that plate-holder! We wore off the points of
our nails, and one of us wore off the edge of her temper;
and used to hit the too faithful custodian a smart rap, to
loosen things. Grief resulted, for if there is anything
equal to the tenacity with which that holder clutches its
plate it is the abruptness with which it lets it go, and the
plate pops off into ruin! That is why I broke several
negatives that might have proven treasures, before we
could even see their features or begin to love them. I
dare say I should have broken many more, had we not
bought a new kind of plate-holder, which has an honest
spring, easily persuaded to release its prisoner; and had
we not discovered that the wide field of usefulness per-
taining to the hairpin extends to photography.

Jane did not risk my impetuous treatment; with her
own fair hands she extricated the plate. " Now," said
she, " the book says we should pour out the developer
into the graduate——"

" That stuff that looks like port wine is the developer,
isn't it? "

" Yes, pyrogallic acid—pyro they call it, with something else in it. The book says to flow it evenly over
the plate."

An Adventure in Photography

She did not dust the plate, because the little book said nothing about dusting. Nor did we blame the dust for our first season's plenteous crop of pinholes; we thought that the plates were poor. Now, we dust scrupulously, and we have a better opinion of plates.

Jane laid the glimmering white plate in the tray, and poured the developer over it; that was what the book commanded, and we obeyed the book, although we sometimes wondered what made the singular appearance of a puddle having dried on the plate; we thought most likely the emulsion had gone wrong. Having finally covered the surface of the plate—the little book prescribed such a limited quantity of fluid that this was rather a feat—she began to sway the dish to and fro. This motion is named rocking; and a number of advantages are ascribed to it. I cannot speak of them with confidence, because, although I rock conscientiously, it has happened that, developing several negatives at once, some little stranger has grown up without rocking, and turned out quite as well as the others. I do not explain this; it simply happened.

But you may be sure we rocked as if the negatives were a first baby, this time. One reason for having a special studio is the necessity of rocking; in the enthusiasm of the moment and the dim light, the scientist is likely to spatter. Jane did not, but Jane was amazingly careful and—amazingly slow! Slowly, carefully she

14

MILKING TIME.

rocked, and strained her eyes to see. The plate was a glimmering rectangle.

What a fascinating thing is the development of a negative! Even at first, when you are at the mercy of your exposure, and if your plate goes wrong, can only helplessly see it go.

"Where's the picture?" said I; but I knew that the picture was invisible, and that the plate would be snow-white for a while; for I, too, had read the little book.

"First, the high lights will come out," said Jane; "the sky comes first, and it will be black, for it is exactly reversed; what is light in the picture is black in the negative, and the very deepest shadow is clear glass. Now look!"

Surely enough, a pall of darkness began to creep, to deepen, to spread; then the outlines of a house, of trees, and cattle came out of the gloom; but the darkness was only a gray darkness, not black; and Jane sighed.

"I am afraid it's over exposed," said she.

"What shall we do?"

"When it is over exposed it is better to use old developer."

"But how can you tell whether you have exposed your negative right?"

"You *can't* tell until it develops."

"But can you stop it *then?* It seems to me that if you have put it in the strong developer it will have

15

taken such a grip on it that it will be all thin before you can take it out."

"The book says it should be immediately put into a tray of water, and then the developer poured back, and some old developer that will not work so fast poured in; but I can't, because we have not any more trays."

So we poured off the developer, and put on the developer that had ushered the first picture into the world— and nothing happened! The cows and the house and the chickens roosting in the trees appeared more and more clearly, but the sky did not acquire any deepening of the desirable black tint, and clear glass appeared in alarming abundance.

Presently a kind of veil spread over the picture. Jane quieted my apprehensions; she said that it was only the proper way for it to look when completed, and she washed it off calmly and put it into a bath of alum. She said that would harden the film. Undoubtedly alum does harden films, but it has not escaped the breath of scandal which loves to blow on every photographic benefactor; it is accused of doing a variety of evil things which I shall not enumerate, because it never did any harm to us. It is a nuisance, but so, frequently, is a baby and many other, in the main, valuable things! The other picture was a cypress brake. I declare I cannot understand to this day why that picture should be so good as it was. Except for thinness (and how many

" THE OTHER PICTURE WAS A CYPRESS BRAKE. "

Showing how we Meant Well

lovely and amiable and gifted people are thin!—I am sure I often wish I were thin myself!) it was a beautiful negative; yet we did not know a rudiment of the art. I can only account for our undeserved success by the same theory that consoles the scientific whist-player when the bumblepuppyist marks up the rubber; namely, that the duffers sometimes, to use the language of the celebrated Mr. Foster, "accidentally hit on plays equal to the best inspirations of genius."

I am quite sure we didn't wash out the developer thoroughly before we put it into the hypo bath; I am equally convinced we did not have the least notion when to take it out of the hypo—and a plain saturated solution of hypo is not an ideal fixing bath—while I have already described our perfunctory washing, afterwards. Happily we did not realize the pitfalls among which we were walking. If we had, we might not have stood our two negatives up on the piano to dry, with such a light heart, and gone to bed so cheerfully.

CHAPTER II

" We are beginning to discover that there is more in
the composing of a picture than we had supposed. It
was our idea that the sun repeated the impression of the
eye: that a pretty scene would look pretty on the glass,
and an ugly one would look ugly. Nothing, it appears,
can be farther from the truth. Everything looks pretty
on the glass. To-day, Jane took a photograph of the
river at the bend.

"It is as sweet a little pastoral as one could ask,
nothing grand, of course, nothing beautiful in any large
sense, but given a peaceful cow grazing on the bank, a
few white dots of sheep under the shade, and what
could be prettier, daintier, than the scene?

"But Jane's picture—it is like a map! The cows and
sheep are pinheads, the river a blur of white. She said
that the objects in the picture had looked small on the
ground-glass, but she somehow hoped that they would
look larger in a negative. Well, they didn't; nothing
looked large except one corner of a fence which had

18

"THE PICTURE OF THE BOYS RESTING IN THE SHADE."

crept unobserved into the landscape, and reared a gigantic shadow on the tiny plain.

" We have tried a number of landscapes ; and either something is the matter with our camera or with us ; for they are all too prosaic for words."

This is an extract from a diary of gloom that we kept the first season. The early stage in the photographic career is wonder and delight at the ability to make any semblance of a picture at all. A camera seems such a witch's toy that to be able to get any obedience whatever from it amazes the beginner.

But this phase passes. Directly, he catches fire from the books which a student buys as soon as he begins to work. The jade Ambition, that harries every artist, and every artisan with the artist's soul, does not disdain our poor dabbler in silver and gelatine and the sun ; she cleverly lures him on her hook. He begins to talk of "pictorial photographs," of composing, of technique, of " pluck " and "brilliancy," and "clearness in the shadows," and "luminous perspective" and " harmonious half-tones," and I know not what of phrases out of the books.

Then the rocks rise out of the river and stab his little pinnace of hope ! This affects me, as being a more unexpected sentence than the assertion that " there is no royal road to photography ; " but it comes to the same thing.

19

An Adventure in Photography

Our theosophist friends do not, I think, grant the privilege of preëxistence to inanimate objects; but we have been tempted to believe that our first camera once was one of those children known as "contrary." The innocent-looking mahogany thing seems to take delight in doing just what we have asked it not to do. Its first mean trick was to snub the middle distance. The middle distance is of a modest turn, and tends to efface itself even when encouraged; our camera pushed it quite out of sight. The foreground flaunted itself in front of a thin strip of perspective that looked to be miles away; above was a wealth of vacant air—for you could not call a uniform gray tint a *sky!* The middle distance seemed to be as cotton planters say they are—in a hole! Nor could we drag it out. If we lowered the focus, the foreground only assumed more alarming proportions, a great expanse of shadowless white ground speckled with grass taking up three-fourths of the picture, and growing and growing like an enraged genius of the " Arabian Nights." If we lifted the lens we got unmitigated sky.

One day, the lightning flash of inspiration visited us—one of us; modesty will not permit me to mention which one—we determined to turn the foreground into middle distance ; out of the nettle, danger, we plucked the flower, safety. Two things are necessary, oh, gentle amateur whom I fondly prefigure to myself following

—·—

these adventures, two things are necessary to capture a middle distance. One thing is to abandon panoramas. In those wide visions all the jewelled hues of sky and cloud and field and iridescent water, lie like fun. The ground-glass picture is no more like the black and white photograph than the fables of the steerage agents about America are like our dear country. Both are very good things in their way, but they have not the same way. You are obliged to translate the witchery of color into plain light and shade; and the translation, like other translations, loses the vivid charm of the original. You fancied yourself looking at a beautiful landscape—behold, in the print, a flat, tame, unrelieved composition; no contrast, no life, no light and shade, no interest. Of course the translation applies to little bits as well as to larger views, but the bits are infinitely easier to translate. Light and shade are more intelligible. And the ground-glass is less deceitful about the picturesqueness of the scene. A lad fishing by the river's edge under a clump of trees, a wagon resting for a nooning by the stream, a figure walking down a country road, a vista of woodland or a glimpse of trees on a river road—these look much the same in colors or in black and white, they retain the same kind of attraction. The middle distance is more manageable in these slight motives, and less missed if it eludes you.

A plan we tried with happy result, is to focus on the interesting object after you have placed it in the centre of your planes; that catches the middle distance, every time. See for yourself, in the picture of the boys resting in the shade. The eye must go find the middle distance; it has no option, the wagon is squarely on the edge of it.

The other necessary thing is to take one's picture either on level ground, or, what is better, slightly up hill. The depth of perspective is vastly helped by a little lift to the angle of view. One reason for our early pictures appearing to be rows of trees or houses growing out of a shelf, was that we made no account of inequalities in the ground; we were as likely to take a view down hill as up.

All this brings me to another trick of the ground-glass. It concerns what the artist calls values. If it were not for a tender conscience and some knowledge of the cost of reproducing photographs, I could fill pages with illustrations of values out of gear, as it were; fences larger than houses, and lop-sided scenery. But what amateur's photograph album has missed such presences?

For a single example, observe, in the picture I sadly submit, the size of those black children in the foreground; they are Gullivers and the women Lilliputians! It is impossible to imagine them ever getting

through that cabin door. They did not look so large on the ground-glass; I am sure they did not. The wide-angle lenses always make distant objects smaller than the eye would make them; they always distort; they pay for their abnormal width of angle by distorting; it is the wages of sin.

The only certain cure for the fault is a good deal like the man's sure cure for a mad dog—he killed the dog! We cut off the distorted parts of the picture—witness the vignette of the washing party. A lens that covers a wider field than your ground-glass will do the same thing permanently and for all your pictures, but it is more expensive.

The question of values, of the harmonious arrangement of a picture, is infinitely expansive. One never solves it; yet its fascinating puzzles reward every success with new ideals and new difficulties. It is not only a question of proportion, it is a question of interest as well. It is a mistake to scatter the interest, just as it is a mistake to sprinkle high lights about too liberally.

Figures, unless they have some plain relation to a landscape, only muddle the story that every picture needs to tell. It need not be a human story; but some phase of the eternal drama every landscape speaks whether we can interpret or no. There is something deeper in the barest and humblest nature than the poets themselves can reach. Wordsworth felt its thrill when he mused over the yellow cowslip, and Burns when he caressed the daisy. Why shall not a photographer be enough of an artist to respect what has awed his betters?

Where a figure is part of a story, that, as our German friends say, is "different again." A lonely old negro in a cotton-field, picking the last picking from the ragged stalks, against a background of his wretched cabin and the setting sun, makes a picture that Ridgway Knight would not disdain.

We have a group of negro boys shooting craps near the mill; the rags and the jollity of those boys were good enough for Brown. It does not harm the picture that there is a dismal cypress slash beyond, for the mill, and the crowd of wagons waiting for the Saturday grist, explain the boys' right to be there. An unfortunate accident to the nose of the best boy has made it impossible, in justice to Jane, to display him. Somehow, in retouching the faces, I did something queer to that child's nose.

In an intermittent fashion, we have made studies of the life of the negro and the "renter." I do not know why a persistent, conscientious effort at a pictorial representation of any people, primitive enough to wear working clothes of their own, should not repay the photographer.

"THOSE BLACK CITIZENS THAT WE CAUGHT WITH THE SHUTTER AT THE BOAT-LANDING."

The Composition of a Picture

But the obstacles are many. You have not only to run down your subject, you have to run down an appropriate *mise en scene*, and—worst job of all!—appropriate lighting. I have been hunting that aged negro in the cotton field with the sunset, for two years: and I have not captured him yet. I have found the cabin and the field and the negro, and the sunset comes to see us every fair day. But I have not been able to collect them simultaneously.

One persistent trial is the previous education of the people. If they had never seen a camera they might be willing to stand where we asked them, but they have all had tintypes taken, and they know that they must face the camera squarely, and hold every muscle rigid and look solemn if they want the picture "to favor them." There they are in the wash-day picture; observe how every woman has assumed her best notion of a good photographic attitude, and how not one of them seems to concern herself further with the washing. Contrast their absorption in the camera with the careless ease of those black citizens that we caught with the shutter, in that picture of the boat landing. In the picture of an Arkansas renter's cabin, in this chapter, there is the same determined sitting for a picture. We tried to arrange those people in the gallery, but it was hopeless; all we could do was to focus in such a way that they should be small. Animals are very valuable in a land-

25

scape; and cows and sheep have not the unmanageable
qualities of human subjects. There is, also, the artist's
own stock device of suggestion. Jane used it in taking
that cottage which you see. She did not want to introduce
a figure, but she did want to show that it was more than a
house, it was a home that she pictured. Do you notice
the little baby-carriage down the walk, quite empty?—
that was Jane's flight of fancy.

It is one of the camera's technical, rather than artistic,
foibles, that it should be such a sad socialist. It makes
out near objects to be far larger than their right of
bulk, and dwarfs all the distant objects, as if the sole
aim of a perspective were to obey Uriah Heep and "be
'umble."

The truth, we take it, is that Jack-of-all-trades lenses
are a good deal like Jack-of-all-trades on a plantation;
they "make out," but they don't make a first-rate job.

The photographer really needs a long-focus lens for
landscapes, and a wide-angle lens for interiors. But
where one finds it as difficult as we have found it to
obtain a long-focus lens, he may be glad to learn the
plan of an English photographer, told to us by an
eloquent clergyman who makes good pictures. The
plan is simply to remove one of the lenses. The single
lens left will make your distance about a quarter larger,
and so far as we can discover you will have no loss of
clearness of definition.

AN ARKANSAS RENTER'S CABIN.

But there are compensations even for the distortions
of the camera. Like conflicting testimony, its lies balance. If it belittles the distant river, it transfigures the
ditch (of the foreground) into a river. Do not those
boys, in the scene before mentioned, appear to be resting by a river bank? They really are beside a "slash"
that runs dry in summer, and could be spanned at high
water by a fallen tree. Little by little we left our seats
of pride and our wide landscapes, and respected the riv-
ulets and the mud puddles. Did you ever attempt a
country road? Just a single figure walking into a
forest vista, that is all—what can be simpler? So we
thought it until we tried to put that simple scene on
our negatives. Then the road unfolded itself in the
most surprising manner, equal to nothing except the
celebrated smile of the Cheshire cat; it expanded and
expanded in front; it contracted and contracted behind; it was not a vista, it was a triangle, and the
obtusest angled triangle in the world, at that!

I had pictured that country road—a beautiful winding
road it was to be—with a symmetrical row of trees,
decreasing slowly from the first to the last, and each
side of the avenue as trim as the picture of a fond
mother's row of boys, with apparently not more than
two years between ages. That is the way trees look in
pictures, but in nature trees cannot be grouped; the near
trees were giants, from which they ran down, not

27

gradually and gracefully, but in jumps and falls, and jumps again. However, thanks to the credulity of the camera, we outwitted it. We selected a part of the road that winds up a slight hill, and we picked out some tender saplings, which we passed off on the lens for gum-trees in their prime; while we worked our way up to some woodland princes in the distance, too big to be entirely slighted. The result was a fairly good picture.

I have not touched on the voluminous subject of lighting; I touch it now with a cautious hand. We have suffered many things from poor lighting; and we shall, in all probability, suffer many more in future; and the reason of our afflictions is the reason of my caution—we do not know how to light a picture. The general impression of the photographer in the dawn of life is that he ought to have the sun at his back. That was our belief. The little book encouraged us in it. And even we could see—after a single trial—that the sun in front will make a neat round white spot on the plate. But the sun on the picture, from behind, makes very unimpressive shadows. So we have preferred side lighting; occasionally, we have dared the sun, by shading the lens. For a long while we could not understand why we had such monotony of lighting; then we read the explanation of it in a book. We have plenty of books, for it has been our custom to buy all the photo-

"JANE'S FLIGHT OF FANCY."

—

graphic books that we have seen in the advertisements ; and to spend time that we might have employed in reading the English classics or the Sunday editions of the newspapers, in poring over them, and admiring to see how much higher fortunes attended other amateurs.

The book told us that a brilliant negative must have brilliant lighting ; high light, dense shadow, masses of light and masses of shadow. At this period we had an ideal photograph. We purchased it in St. Augustine, Florida. It represented a scene on the Ocklawaha River. The shadows were dark as purple-toned paper will go, the river glittered from shadow to white light, and the sky was white as the driven snow. We struggled after a white sky as earnestly at that season as we are now struggling for tints and cloud effects. Our negatives were so thin that high lights were craved by us with a yearning longing. We took the book's advice and lit our little world from the side. But though we had side lighting, those desirable masses of light and those rich, long shadows did not appear. Sometimes a picture that the ground-glass showed us flooded with radiance, appeared in print speckled in white patches like a barred Plymouth Rock hen. Trees dappled with light may look beautiful in a forest, in a photograph they merely look streaked.

" We photograph at the wrong hour of the day," pronounced Jane, solemnly ; " *what* is the right one ? "

29

An Adventure in Photography

Long since, Jane herself had discarded the little book; I don't know which one of us threw it into the fire, though I know which one was the more likely to do such a thing. It matters not, it was gone, and Jane now pinned her faith to "The Photographic Times Annual" and that distinguished amateur, General Joseph Brown. I can't say whether it was General Joseph or a lesser idol that explained shadows to us; whoever he be, he will please accept this intimation. We are still grateful to him for his clear definition of shadow. The sun, high at noonday, does not cut any figure as a silhouette painter; the long shadows come early in the morning or late in the afternoon. Just before sunset one can sometimes catch an effect as if the objects were outlined in light—as in these sheep. I am told an equally fascinating but different charm pertains to the sunrise light; we shall preserve that early stroll and those golden exhalations of the dawn for our old age, when we may enjoy them more; at present we do not rise at six for anything less than a railway despot or sickness in the house.

There is a fugitive, subtle quality about this whole business of lighting. It reminds me of my first parasol. I was so little that I did not know where the sun was, and I kept shifting my new splendor from side to side as I saw people coming or going, in as many minds about my parasol as poor Lemuel Barker was in about his fork, when he first dined in Boston.

30

"AT SUNSET."

The Composition of a Picture

The shadows in a picture are so altered and disguised by color that, although we make an opera-glass of our hands, and squint up our eyes in the best approach we know to the artistic formula, we never quite determine what to expect of the lighting until we see it on the negative.

As for half-tones, a picture is a crude, harsh thing without nature's exquisite gamut of gradations in tint, the like of which we can only image in black and white by half-tones; yet they seem as hard to obtain as the truth about the negro. And the deceitful ground-glass is in its element, suppressing neutral grays by every lie in color that there is. Foliage has to be carefully studied, and is likely to turn out a muddy black after all your pains. However, foliage is as much a matter of development as of lighting. And here comes in one of the mournfulest features of photography. You need to know the whole trade at once. Vain is the truest and most ingenious artist's eye if you jar your tripod, or leave your plate-holder on the ground, or forget to remove your slide, or drop your cap and it rolls away, or neglect to turn your slide after the picture is taken, and thus take two pictures on one plate, or have the wee-est crevice for light to slip into your bellows, or do one of twenty possible (and *we* should say probable) wrong things; and after you have held your breath and taken your picture correctly, ten to one you will muddle

31

it somehow in the development, to say nothing of the multitudinous perils of printing!

Indeed, I have often thought that the devil would have had a fairer chance in that memorable tussle of his with Job, had he only known about photography. It was invented long after his day, the better for the testy patriarch; for, could Satan have sent the old gentleman out with a model five-by-eight camera, tugging eight or ten plate-holders, on a warm Judean day, trying to get an instantaneous view of one of the comforters galloping away on his Arab steed, with a drop shutter that hitched in the drop; or could he have inveigled him into attempting portraits of the children that should satisfy his wife, boils would have seemed a mild discipline in comparison. At least, that is the opinion of a good friend of ours. He says, "I have had boils, and I have had a camera; and boils are not in it."

CHAPTER III

A MAKESHIFT STUDIO

WE had not been photographing two weeks before we outgrew the corner of the dining-room and set up a studio. It is a small room off the kitchen, about twelve by fourteen in dimensions. Up North we have had a regular dark room and printing room constructed for us, with running water, gas, and the like conveniences; but our Southern studio is much more inexpensive, and I don't know but that we make quite as good pictures in it.

You remember the poet:

> "What and how great the virtue and the art,
> To live on little with a thankful heart."

We have no running water nearer than the kitchen pump. Instead, on the common kitchen table which we have bought for a developing table there is a dripping pan, in the northwest end of which a dipper handle is soldered, making an admirable funnel. The funnel passes through a hole in the table. A tub stands on the floor under the funnel, which catches considerable of the waste water—we should not be amateur

3   33

photographers if it caught all. Next to the pan is a box surmounted by a common water bucket with a wooden cock; so that we can turn the water on to our negatives at any rate we desire, from a trickle to full speed. The water runs off the negative into the pan and through the funnel. The whole outfit cannot have cost more than three dollars, including the table. There is a shelf above the table, and a kind of ell to the table on the right, built by one of the plantation carpenters. On the opposite side of the room a printing table runs the whole length of the wall, with shelves above and below. When we need shelves, and there is no carpenter available, any small box will make two shelves. On one pair of box shelves is our library; a large packing box holds the negative boxes and the printing frames, while a great chest has our paper, and the blankets that serve us for backgrounds when we take portraits. The studio is lighted frankly by two large panes of yellow glass, and on the sly by white light which sifts through unperceived cracks about the door or the ceiling. The room was originally whitewashed, which is a great help to the light.

It is not the easy matter that it may seem to make a dark room. I stop up the orange window with a shutter that we have had built for the purpose. I tack thick felt paper over every crack that I can discover, I hang black cloth over the doors. I hope that it is

because I have been in the room so long that I seem to
see so much, in spite of this toil. I appeal to Jane.
"White light just *streaming* in, isn't it?" says Jane,
cheerfully.

I can see the odious white walls glimmering, but it is
one thing to be aware of your failures, quite another to
have them flaunted in your face by one from whom
you expected sympathy; I answer with dignity that I
can't see my hand before my face.

"No more can I," says Jane, still cheerful; "but I
can almost read the labels on those bottles opposite."

To which I reply that I am going to develop in that
room, by that light, and see what will come of it.
Nothing comes of it; I do not know why the negatives
are not fogged, as Jane expects (in my soul, I rather
expect it, too!), but they are not; and Jane enters in the
book of our experience: "Plates developed under cover
can bear a remarkable amount of white light."

Above our developing table hangs a noble lantern,
which has red and yellow and white light. It is from
Mr. Carbutt, and I think it cost six dollars, and it is
cheap at the price. And although we do not develop
with it, regularly, now, we often find it very useful.

We have a theory in regard to lanterns. For a long
time we used to wonder whether our recurring misad-
ventures with lanterns were due to the lanterns or to
our own stupidity, which we both admit was versatile

35

and persistent. Our first lantern was the size of one's fist, and was called The Gem or The Jewel or some such pretty name. It disturbed the sacred blackness with hardly a gleam of red light, and a very efficient smell of oil. It does not harm a negative, not in the least. The negative takes its own course for weal or woe, not affected by anything, because the operator sees nothing of it until it comes out of the fixing bath with its character formed for life. We can putter over it, intensify or reduce, help or hinder a little, but as a whole the die is cast. Occasionally, with this lantern, we poured the developer on unevenly and made rings on the plate, or we made a slight mistake in our tray positions, and the rapidly thinning negative, instead of visiting the density solution, was popped into the deadly alkali waiting for the instanticties. It will be seen that it was safer for the negative for us to stand aside and let nature take her course, unhampered. When we got anything that would print we were thankful; when we didn't, we were not surprised. It was a splendid lantern for a philosopher, it kept him always in training!

Our next venture was a lantern pluming itself on its innocence. It was an ascetic lantern; it did not pretend to give much light; but it declared light to be a mortal sin in a dark room, anyhow; the less light on the plate the better; the desideratum was to have no dangerous and disagreeable oil about. The lantern in question had no oil; it burned a candle. We used it twice. Any reader of this book who desires a perfectly safe dark lantern that will never explode can have the before-mentioned treasure by applying to us, and sending a suitable box for transportation. Express to be collected at the other end.

Our third lantern was bought because we read in *Scribner's Magazine* about some one who spared his skies and painted in the reluctant foliage with strong developer. He was accustomed to linger long over his negatives, and they were of surpassing beauty.

"He couldn't *see* to paint by our lantern," observed Jane.

"Anything on earth might happen to a negative by our lantern and we not know it," I agreed, sadly.

"Why don't you get another lantern?" said Madonna; "I read a beautiful advertisement——"

"*These* lanterns were both in beautiful advertisements," interrupted my partner, before I could make the same remark; and she added, in a bitter, bitter tone which pained me—for I hate to witness the ravages of photography on that gentle spirit, but the little book, as we say in Arkansas, "had done its do:"—"You can't believe anything they say in advertisements or in the photograph books, either!"

"Why, Jenny, you said you liked Burton's Printing so much."

An Adventure in Photography

"I don't mean him," said Jane; "I don't mean any of the books to professionals; I mean the amateur books, photography-made-easy kind of books. But we might buy another lantern, I suppose. It could not well be worse. That is one compensation."

We bought a lantern. We left the nature of the luminary to the judgment of the St. Louis firm that supplied us with photographic implements. They sent us very good drugs and other things, and we trusted them. I would not say that they betrayed our trust. The lantern that they sent gave a fair amount of light, and, until it exploded, served us well. Neither did it explode without warning; it used to make hissing and snorting noises, like a person in a fit of some kind, and the flame would flare up unpleasantly. This naturally was sure to happen when we were at the most critical juncture in the evolution of the negative; consequently we were forced to continue, but we felt at a frightful risk: and we always stood ready to flee for our lives.

We gave it air, we set it on a high, dry box; but whatever we did, the instant we were well into business, "Whir! pshutt! hiss-s-s!" it gurgled and sputtered, and the flame began to caper, and we knew that we were juggling with doom! On the whole, it was a relief when it did its worst, and we threw the fragments into the Black River.

I cannot recall anything about our next lantern, ex-

38

WHERE WE THREW THE LANTERN.

cept that it was beneath contempt. Then, saying nothing, Madonna sent to Philadelphia for the Carbutt lantern, which has been a comfort to us ever since. But in no time the Carbutt lantern began to flicker; and we almost gave up hope. We examined the lantern and a common lamp, seeking for the principles of combustion. We did not find many, but we found enough to be sure that a lantern standing on a table, generally a wet table to the bargain, does not get enough air. We hung the Carbutt lantern on the wall, and it has never flickered since. That is our theory about lanterns. Hang them!

As I have said, however, we do not develop by the Carbutt lantern; we light it to give additional illumination to the room; we develop by a common lantern, placed on a stand, outside our orange glass window, or by a common white light kerosene lamp, without any screen whatever.

With such a light there is no hardship in developing. One can read the labels as well as see the bottles in any part of the room. Only with such a light, moreover, is it possible for an inexperienced photographer to rescue injured negatives.

Most of our apparatus we have built on plans culled from the "Mosaics" (a capital annual of which one cannot easily speak too highly), or from some other photographic journal. That pile of boxes embodies one idea. They are, you will observe, puttied at the joints and lined with white oilcloth. The oilcloth has no seams, and the tacks that secure it are all on the outside of the box. Thus you have a perfectly innocent, deep tray, for toning or washing. And they are so cheap that one may have plenty of them. Our hypo we keep on a stand by itself. It has its own measuring glass, its own wooden stick for stirring, and its own boxes. Thanks to our exclusiveness, hypo has wrought very little mischief among us. We discovered very soon that the fixing of negatives by laying them flat on their backs in the hypo, is attended with many disadvantages. Any sediment in the bath will get on to the film of the negative, and there is not such quick fixing as when the plate stands upright. For our hypo bath we have flat boxes for prints, but for negatives, a deep box lined with oilcloth, with strips of smooth wood on opposite sides. Each strip has little grooves to hold the negative firmly to its work. We saw out the grooves with a tiny saw we have, and use half a dozen of the tools that come in a handle; and make considerable fuss over the matter; but I suspect that an ordinary penknife could do the business just as well.

We have a quantity of porcelain trays and rubber and enamelled-tin trays, and we did have glass trays until they broke—the average life of the glass tray is two weeks—but for washing and fixing nothing excels the boxes with the oilcloth lining.

A Makeshift Studio

I don't understand how professional photographers get along without boiling water for washing; we always use it, and when the weather grows too warm to depend on the kitchen supply, we have both an alcohol lamp and a wee oil stove.

We could not carry on the business without a dozen or so of printing frames, and almost as many glass graduates of various sizes, and a beautiful pair of apothecaries' scales. For a while we used to keep our negatives in a box of polished wood which cost us two dollars; but when our large following of the camera, outgrew their quarters, we stored them (in envelopes which we made ourselves out of yellow Manila paper) in a cast-off packing-box that did not cost us a cent. The envelopes are marked legibly, and bear the name and developing pedigree of the negative within; and they stand in rows in the box with their names in sight, the bromide negatives in one box, the platino-type in another, and the albumen in a third.

Any facts of interest in the career of a negative are written on the envelope. There is a semicircular portion cut out of the front of each envelope to facilitate handling. All this sounds very orderly; and the little mottoes with which one of us adorned the walls of the studio, on an idle afternoon, are of the sternest moral cast, like "To-Day is Ours"—naturally the favorite of the procrastinating partner—but the painful truth is

that our studio is the most determinedly untidy room
on the plantation, bar none! As I have intimated
before, we are coming to believe that occult forces
sway matter. It is easy to imagine intelligences too low
and mean even to be allowed in pigs or rats or a certain little black and white brute shunned by all, rul-
ing *things*, totally depraved things. These "obsessed"
creatures swarm in our studio. They love to bewitch
the tub, which promptly springs a leak and floods our
floor with poison; this is to lure the cat and the dogs
(good, well-bred, high-descended, imported dogs that
cost money) to an awful death! They hope, also, that
the baneful fluids will trickle through the cracks of the
floor and flow off under the house into the back-yard,
and that Jane's special pets, the high and well-born
hens, imported in the shell, at vast expense, may drink
and die. They would fairly revel in that!

Pending our gradual destruction, they do their best
to fill the room with dust and to suggest to the cook
that it would make a good storeroom.

Being printing room, dark room, and pharmacy, we
have so many traps about that we must be tidy as a
sailor to keep any space vacant in the middle of the
room or on the tables. We are not tidy as a sailor, we
are more like the inhabitants of Italy whom Mark
Twain found "always washing and never clean!"

In consequence, during the photographic season, we

A Makeshift Studio

have weekly seasons of house-cleaning that take up almost as much time as regular work; and I am at the point of taking an apprentice to teach him the business, just as country lawyers teach law, beginning with sweeping and dusting and washing, and so climbing up to abstract principles. The only difficulty will be to find the apprentice.

43

CHAPTER IV

THE NEGATIVE, ITS MARK: A LONG CHAPTER, INCLUD-
ING THE PHOTOGRAPHIC SKY, CAN WE SAVE IT?
WHITE LIGHT DEVELOPMENT, ORTHOCHROMATIC
PLATES, FILMS, THE VARIOUS PLATES AND DEVEL-
OPERS, AND THE LIMITATIONS OF THE INSTANTA-
NEOUS SHUTTER

A CELEBRATED whist expert, at the close of a lucid treatise on "the noblest game," remarks something to this effect: "These rules hold good where there are not exceptions, but it should be borne in mind that whist is everlastingly exceptional!"

So is a negative. There is nothing regular or moral about the conduct of a gelatine dry plate. The only thing to be expected from it is a surprise. You are told that a negative belongs to three classes, the under exposed, the over exposed, and the normally exposed; but you are not told that the chances are about one in a hundred that your particular negatives will hit on a normal, proper, perfect exposure; and you are not told that you may easily contrive to get all three exposures in varying degrees into one negative. Nevertheless, my friend, you may and you will.

44

The Negative, its Mark

An over-exposed plate has plenty of detail, but jumps out of the developer in such a hurry that it does not get its density on before it is all out; it is thin, the shadows are poor, there are no high lights, the sky is a dull half-tone; it looks like a lead-pencil drawing.

The under exposed are the reverse of this; in them the half-tones are wanting, there are violent blacks and whites, detail is masked in shadow; they look harsh and unfinished. Under-exposed negatives come up slowly; they hang back and must be whipped to their work with alkalies, and after a certain point they jib, and are no more to be moved than a jibbing horse. The doctors differ in regard to them. Most hold that there is nothing more on the plate, and it is hopeless to get it out. But there is another school maintaining that the sun makes all the picture; it is but the weakness of the developer and the ignorance of the operator that hinders the luring out of the details. We are not scientific, Jane and I, and we profess no opinion; we simply know that eikonogen will get more out of a sullen plate than either pyro or hydroquinone.

The normally exposed negative should (according to the books—*we* never have had any such children of light) appear in about a minute and a half; it should develop harmoniously and evenly (ours never did); the clouds in the bright sky, and the delicate shadows of the child's white frock forming and shaping themselves in

sweet communion with the leaves of the dense shrubbery and the half-tints of the lawn.

The over-exposed ought never to act like the under-
exposed. There, again, we were vanquished by exceptions; it was as easy for our under-exposed plates to
thin out like over-exposed plates as it was for half the
picture to "flash," while the other half didn't stir. We
supposed, for our comfort, that a negative could be thin
or it could be dense, it could not be both. *Ours* can!
We have had negatives stained with pretty nearly
every photographic crime; that were thin without
detail, and dense without contrast; and made as unmanageable bromides as they did anything else. We
have had under exposures as thin as over exposures.
Our over exposures, on the other hand, have loved to
act, under our gentle first developer, like under-exposed
negatives, thus inveigling us on and on into stronger
and stronger developer; then they would pretend that the
developer was too strong for them, and come up in a flash,
with a fog for the sky and a smudge for the shadows.

During the greater part of our first year it was a
sheer matter of chance how our negatives should turn
out. We knew that they were under-exposed, if we
could not coax a mark out of the plate; we supposed
that they were over-exposed if they were thin, but with
plenty of detail; and when they were thin without detail
we gave it up!

A GOOD LIGHTING.

The Negative, its Mark

Such a wild dream as stopping an over-exposed plate
on its way to ruin, never occurred to us; it was the ruin
that revealed to us, first, that it *was* over-exposed. We
had a one-solution developer that came with the camera,
and when it was gone—and how quickly it went, that
developer, that told us on its outside that it ought
to develop fifty plates!—we sent for some more, and
the sad scene was repeated. For, doubtless, some wise
reason, the amateur, in his darkling first experiences,
succeeds in making, now and then, a really good negative. *He* doesn't make it, it makes itself! Generally,
he spoils it in the varnishing. But it keeps him from
entire despair. Out of at least half a dozen boxes of
plates we secured four good negatives. That first
winter our dark room was a school for the perseverance
of the saints. I used to see the halo, sometimes, so
distinctly encircling Jane's brow that I almost feared for
the plates! I admired the sight—particularly on those
occasions when I put the plates in wrong side up, and
they were developed weirdly in patches. What a
beautiful quality is patience! Can we pray for any
fairer gift for our nearest and dearest? If they only
have it, it is not so much matter about us. I am
willing that Jane should have patience for two.

Our first gleam of light in our murky ignorance was
the discovery that an under-exposed plate may have the
right to be thin. The action of light in making con-

trast increases up to a certain point, then it decreases in apparently the same ratio.

"Don't you reckon, then, that those negatives we exposed so short a time, and yet they were so thin, were under-exposed after all?" said Jane.

"I reckon," I answered.

Our next discovery concerned the whole nature of exposure; we came to it slowly and painfully, of our own motion. Later we were confirmed in it by the authorities.

Jane expressed it in one sentence, not a stiff, grammatical, rhetorical sentence, but one full of rugged truth: "We have got to look at the *things* we take, as well as the light," said she.

You cannot (at least *we* cannot) expect to find a stupid scene monotonously lighted, and to enchant it into a brilliant negative by simple conjuring of development. We came to divide our subjects into very much the three classes of M. Londe, namely, "Subjects which have a perfect harmony of tone gradation; subjects which present strong contrasts and oppositions; and subjects which have not enough contrast and opposition, and are consequently weak."

After we took the blacksmith shop, with its blazing white walls and road, and its dark, dark water-oak tree and its dusky depths within, of a sunny morning, we concluded that a little over-exposure would have had a

48

A BAD LIGHTING.

softening, soothing effect on such exaggerated chiaro-oscuro. A few seconds extra exposure would have saved an hour or two puttering with a reducer. After we took any number of monotonous, palely lighted pictures, it occurred to us that a shorter exposure would have done no harm, and might have given the scene's weak character a fillip.

And then it was that we came upon the whole subject clearly discussed, and all the obscure places illuminated by good sense. We found it in a little book on the development of the negative, by the Rev. W. H. Burbank. Mr. Burbank advised over-exposures for harsh contradictory subjects, short exposures for tame subjects, and normal exposures for harmonious subjects.

He did not need to tell us of the enormous increase in the radiant energy of light during the summer months; we had discovered that in the surest possible way, at the expense of less than two dozen plates.

By this time we were so far along that we had ambitious dreams of remedying exposures. To a skilful operator no exposure is hopeless that has been exposed enough; the only unpardonable sin in taking a picture is not to expose enough; and some of us hope one day for a developer that will compassionate even that.

Our first real advance in development was made when we read Burton's recommendation of the tentative method.

49

An Adventure in Photography

—

"Why, isn't it perfectly sensible?" said Jane; "you put your negative into a very weak developer to try it; then if it is not strong enough put in a little more density, and then add the alkali drop by drop, changing the proportions to suit the case. I mean to try it."

We have tried it ever since, with continually increasing confidence in the method and gratitude to the first suggester.

We always put the plate into the plate-holder in the first place in absolute darkness. Moonlight, however, does not seem to affect the gelatine. Several times we have been obliged to put in our plates by moonlight, and there was no ill effect. When the time for development comes we remove the plates from the holders and slip them into the trays prepared for them, with a bath of developer. Then we cover them with stiff pasteboard or wooden covers, painted black. All so far in total darkness. Before we put our plates into the holders, and before we put them into the negative baths, we always carefully dust them off; we also wipe the inside of our camera with a damp cloth (a bit of valuable advice that we obtained in the "Photographic Annual" of 1890, from O. P. Havens); we find it simpler and less wearing on the moral nature to brush off our pinholes in advance than to stop them out afterwards.

Since we took a fond farewell of our one-solution

developer we have had no Procrustean system of
development. Our treatment varies according to the
exposure, the subject, and the plate. Taking assuredly
under-exposed subjects, we should be likely to soak
them in a weak solution of alkali (a five-per-cent. solution, let us say) such as welcomes the instantaneous
negatives. Taking them out of the alkali we should see
what eikonogen or para-midophenol could do for their
obtuse nature, beginning with a weak solution. and
gradually adding the alkali and then a little more
density.

For ordinary exposures we like to start with a weak
solution of the developer, whatever it may be, adding
the alkali very cautiously, developing for detail first and
then putting the negative into the density solution to
obtain density. For undoubted over-exposures we start
always with a weak solution of the developer, without
any alkali, and add very little, if any, alkali. We have
developed negatives in the eikonogen solution alone,
adding no alkali, letting the sulphite of sodium, combined with the developer, do the whole alkali work.
We prefer restraining with the developer, weakening it
with water, rather than trying to hold it back by
bromides, but bromides are better than old developer.
Water makes a negative softer, so that a good way with
a negative known to have harsh contrasts is to soak it
in a tray of water before development.

51

An Adventure in Photography

Old developer is the favorite of many photographers; it is not ours, we being willing to make affidavit that it tends to too great contrasts, to masking the half-tints and to mussing the shadows. Nevertheless, we keep a little always on hand. But we do it in the spirit of those stern temperance people, who keep a bottle of brandy in the house for sickness; we don't really think it does any good, but we are afraid to be without it.

An over-exposed negative will sometimes become a delightful picture by slow development, using alternate trays of the alkali and the developer proper. We have obtained excellent results by weakening the developer only in the alkali, giving full strength of eikonogen.

We have come to prefer a slight over-exposure, as it insures the whole story about the landscape, every stick and stone of it. But, to obtain the whole truth about the foliage, one must expose a scene too long for the sky and the brightly lighted portions.

In the normal exposures we begin with a weak developer, but it is weakened by water, and has both alkali and eiko or other developing agent in it, in the normal proportions, while the over-exposed has either no alkali or the merest trace of it, and the under-exposed has more alkali than the normal developer contains. Yet even here the subject casts foregleams of advice. Where the under exposure has been deliberate, to

"DUCKS GOT AWAY."

(Orthochromatic sky.)

secure more contrast in a landscape of commonplace lighting, a slow development with a restrainer will help the contrast and bring out the half-tones.

After we have covered our negatives—we develop several at a time on account of the brevity of life and the length of development—we wait perhaps five minutes, and then take a peep by the yellow light at the first one. Sometimes the picture will be distinctly visible. More often only a little darkening in the upper side will hint the dawning of the sky. We shake the tray a little, add what the case seems to require in the way of developer, and go on to the next object of solicitude. Presently we return to our first, which now has blocked out a shadowy, unreal landscape, with black sky and white trees. Here and there, the details begin to shape themselves, patches of high light on the fences, glints on the leafage, fleecy clouds in the sky. We lift the little tray, carry it boldly to the yellow light, and examine it.

" It is coming," pronounces the operator; " nice sky!"

" Anything else but sky visible? How is the foliage?" asks the other operator.

" Dense," is the mournful answer, "it hasn't put out a twig yet. I am going to paint it with concentrated developer, to try to spare the sky; everything else is coming all right, good detail. Only the foliage sticks fast."

53

An Adventure in Photography

Alas! as she works, she wearies of painting and adds a more powerful pusher, and little by little the animated, lovely sky grows blacker and blacker—which means, eventually, whiter and whiter—until it is resolving itself into cloudless, blank, unshaded space.

" How shall we save our beautiful skies ? " we used to demand pathetically of the universe in general ; and the universe didn't bother itself to answer.

We consulted all the books. That is, all the books that we could find. They recommended an orthochromatic plate. They were sad, not to say cynical, with regard to skies on ordinary plates. Burton said that only a mere trace of a sky appears, and recommended " printing in " skies.

From the books we went to the professional and the amateur photographers of our acquaintance, including two skilful and modest photographers in Davenport, and one superior boy in a Boston establishment. One of the Davenport photographers favored his sky by tilting the tray, and developing the foliage and grass, leaving the sky only an intermittent wave.

The celebrated photographer who told his experiences in *Scribner's Magazine* about this time, painted *his* foliage, or any under-exposed parts, in strong developer, using a camel's-hair brush, and flowing the brushed portions immediately, to guard against any line of demarcation showing.

A SUMMER SKY.

(A carbutt eclipse sky.)

The Negative, its Mark

We followed—as usual—the advice of all, and let the different theories fight it out for themselves. We use orthochromatic plates, and like them; but both of us having been born and bred in New England and trained to respect the truth, we have to add that we have obtained every whit as good skies from the ordinary Carbutt B, or Special, or Eclipse, or the Seeds 23, 24, or 26, or the Eagle Lightning plates, as from the orthochromatic plates. In the group of sky negatives that is given in this chapter one was taken on orthochromatic and the other two on ordinary plates, and we could not honestly decide between the skies. But there are other advantages of the orthochromatic plates that endear them to us, notably their rendering of half-tints and values.

We find that in nine cases out of ten we can get a sky out on the negative if there was a sky on the plate. And it is our opinion that ninety-nine times out of a hundred, when there is anything going on in the sky, it will be repeated on the plate. And you can't really ask a negative to make up a sky out of its head!

Mr. Cramer, I see, asserts that the ordinary plate cannot take white clouds, it can only take dark ones. But, "speaking with respect," we have had ordinary plates, without seeming to strain themselves at all, take white clouds in a dark sky, or, rather, in a sky just off the white tint.

An Adventure in Photography

At first these pretty skies appeared on thin negatives, but we have, for a long time, been getting them almost as freely on strong negatives. But we have never found them on negatives developed very quickly, and, indeed, they never favored us until we used the tentative method.

We give our skies every luxury and advantage in our power. We develop them slowly and carefully. After they are out, we paint the greenery and the distance with special developer, but we develop in developer that will not harm the skies. We put the negative in a tray of water, development being advanced sufficiently so far as the high lights and half-tones are concerned, and then we paint the deep shadows, washing off the edges by rocking the tray after every painting. One should be careful, however, for the strong developer, even without the "pusher" (which is a sort of hair-trigger explosive, likely to shoot the owner) is no promoter of recklessness, but a quick-tempered and sensitive nature that must be spoken fair.

If, in spite of brushing until incipient fog warns "hands off," the foliage will not come, all is not lost. Give the foliage its protracted bath of stronger developer instead of its quick flashes of the strongest; it will come out with all the delicate gradations that you are seeking. True, the sky, the charming, varied, natural sky, will be darkened to blackness; but it is not a case of lost,

A GIPSY CAMP.

(Seeds 26 sky.)

only of temporary disappearance. We develop our negatives to the last shrub. If the sky has gone off in a fit of sulks, we bring it back! After fixing, we prepare a small quantity of Farmer's Solution for reducing negatives, place the negative in a tray of fresh water, tilt the water away from the sky, and neatly wash that sky with a half-inch camel's-hair brush. The result is an almost immediate reduction. You have to be cautious lest the reducing solution trickle down on to any other part of the plate. But so far as reducing the high lights goes, it is a complete success.

We had an interior that we liked, but it had a window that was simply a splash of dead white. We reduced the window and the tablecloth of the table. The vine on the other side of the window appeared, and a dab of out-of-focus scenery beyond, likewise the pattern of the tablecloth.

Negatives too sharply contrasted can be safely and evenly reduced by adding the solution drop by drop to a water-bath, and rocking the negative therein. The treatment for a negative is a good deal like the treatment for a child. Jane and I, having had nephews and nieces upon whom to experiment at a safe distance, are naturally full of theories about the proper training of children. We are not hampered by the bewildered discouragement that besets the mother of six, who has tried a promising assortment of theories and found them all going the wrong way. But we know how she feels; we have had much the same experience with our negatives. I could not lay my hand on my heart and tell the confiding buyer of this book that any treatment would save any particular negative. No, negatives are like children, every one must have an individual treatment of its own, based on an individual study of its character. To deal justly by a negative, the operator must know the character of the exposure, the nature of the subject, the make of the plate, and the peculiarities of the developer. He must watch every mood narrowly, and adapt his action. If the picture hang back sullenly, he must coax it (not *drive* it forward) with minute doses of alkali ; if it is in too great a hurry, he must restrain it with a weaker alkali developer and more of the density solution. He must always be ready to give it a dose of bromide, or citrate and water. And he must have a patience that is willing to sit out the evening rather than be conquered by the naughty child. Often an under-exposed negative, that would be ruined by a concentrated developer surprising its crude nature, will develop harmoniously if given plenty of time and a gradually strengthened developer.

When a negative has nearly developed, it is said to be a good plan (I say " said," because we really cannot decide whether our negatives, so developed, are a pinhead's worth better than any of the others. It is one of

A SOUTHERN KITCHEN.

—

the examples of the hiatus between fact and theory to which I have referred—all mothers will understand me) to take such a negative and let it rest quietly in a tray of clean water. The theory supposes the water to make, with the developer already in the negative film, a kind of dilute developer, that will work slowly while a particle remains. It is a very nice, plausible supposition. Our only objection to it is the paltry one of experience, already mentioned.

As the development proceeds, the next pressing question is, When shall we stop?

Jane and I used to discuss that question innumerable times at first. We were always stopping our development before the details were fairly out, for fear of fog from over-development—a disaster, by the way, that has never once befallen us.

I don't know any better advice than Burton's and Burbank's and, I think, Abney's, to stop development when all detail seems to be out, and the image is visible on the glass side, the high lights showing plainly.

Our well-lighted dark room has scared away this early ogre. We can see, now, when the details have come; we used to have to guess.

During the development we soon began to observe the influence of temperature. If the weather is too cold, your negatives, oh, gentle photographing brother, will stick; if it is too warm, they will race at a frantic pace. The ideal temperature is from sixty-five to, seventy degrees.

Another trouble for negatives is not so easily remedied as temperature. Some plates, or, to be just, some developers, and particularly my dear and valued eikonogen, are untrusty about density. They assure you solemnly that they have taken all the density that they need, that their little insides cannot bear one atom more, and you believe them. You lift up the negative; it is beautiful! Brilliant, well-balanced, richly contrasted, it makes your heart swell with pride! You wash it off, reflecting on the brief space of time that it has taken for you to become a master of your art, and you put it proudly into the hypo. You expect to gaze upon the same picture again when you take it out—which is all you know about it! Out of that hypo will come the pale ghost of your superb negative! You will hardly be able to believe it the same. In this way eikonogen, which has almost every other virtue as a developer, has caused us cruel moments. How many times have we done what Faust saved his soul by not doing, and said "to the passing moment (of the development): 'Stay, thou art too fair!'" But that particular moment never did stay; it made haste to hustle its beauty off in the hypo, and tempt us to quarrel and use unseemly reproaches the one to the other, because the development had not been prolonged.

The Negative, its Mark

I have noticed in many arts that there comes a time when the causes for failure seem to lose their potency. It is not any one thing that the student does after he has mastered the trade, that stops them; they simply do not harass him any more. A good cook cannot teach all her skill. She does not know why many things happen, herself; she puts a name to reasons why that which nearly ruined her dainties now disturbs them no more; but it is only a form of words; in her secret soul she will admit as much, and say: " It is all in the knack." Word of magic! who knows what it means?

There is a " knack " about development. Once acquired, the caprices of negatives become harmless as the piping of chickens; and yet one hardly can say *how* they were overquelled. I think that we try to get too much density with these exaggerating developers, leaving a margin for the future, as one does in fish stories and horse trades. I have seen negatives that seemed nearly shrouded in density, that looked ruined, in fact, come out of the hypo clear and sharp, and give first-rate prints! And I have seen a negative that did nothing of the sort, and came out of his bath the same sooty fellow. In this event there is nothing for it but reducing. Reducing is safe and sure. It is another pair of sleeves, as the French say, to intensify.

We still keep the intensifying solutions with which we ruined several promising young negatives, whose

—

only fault was that they were not intense. We do not keep the negatives. Neither do we use the intensifier. If we have a thin negative, we print under tissue paper or we print bromides. The bromide loves the thin negative, for its nature is to increase contrast.

Intensifying is generally a dangerous performance, sometimes fatal to the operator, for it uses deadly poisons, and it is almost invariably disappointing, wherefore we have no more of it.

Having developed the negative, the washing-bath is the next step. Some of those people who hold to the doctrine of increase of trouble being necessarily a proportionate, or disproportionate, increase in excellence; tender photographic consciences that are sure a thing must be helpful if it can only be made enough of a bother, will have it that the developer is nearly as tenacious of its grip as the hypo, and should be washed off for almost as long a time. They assert that it mixes with the hypo, and goes on developing at a prodigious rate until a perfectly developed negative comes out of the fixing-bath a ruined child. They have the example of the apparently dense eikonogen negatives that emerge from the hypo with all the appearance of over-development, for an argument. The remedy, of course, is unlimited washing.

Jane, who is naturally painstaking and conscientious, looked on this theory with favor. But after I had

developed a dozen or so eikonogen negatives and found
no trouble with density if I used carbonate of potash
instead of carbonate of soda, and in all the cases had
merely rinsed them off with the perfunctory haste of a
child washing its own face, it did occur to me that there
was a leak somewhere in that stately theory.

As usual, we compromised with our experience.
Now we rinse the negatives off in running water, but
before this is done they have generally soaked in a tray
of water for twenty minutes.

Our negatives washed, they are fixed in hyposulphite
of soda. I suppose that a chapter might be written
about fixing methods, especially were the writer to dip
into ancient history, and the tragedies of cyanide of
potassium. At first we used a bath of a simple saturated solution of hypo. An alum bath followed. Then
we were scared by the evil reports regarding alum, and
used the hypo bath alone. It did well enough until the
warm weather came, and our plates began to "frill," and
to show signs of intending to slip off the glass entirely.
We iced the developer, we iced the hypo; but ice is not
plentiful enough on a plantation for us to ice the hogshead of washing water. Then we came upon Carbutt's
formula for a fixing-bath. We found it in the dark
room of the amiable professional photographer in
Davenport, already mentioned. He had used it with
good results. We have used it ever since. It will be

found among the formulæ at the end of this chapter. Some tried and true formulæ will be given for amateurs who wish that kind of thing.

The Carbutt fixing-bath is the Seeds also; and, indeed, is a favorite often given in the books. It deserves its popularity, giving a film tough, glassy, and smooth—a film to be trusted in warm water. We have used the acid sulphite bath, also. There seems little to choose between the two.

After fixing in the first hypo bath, it is a good thing to wash the negative off in running water, which will clear the plate of any sediment which may have adhered to it, and then to fix for twenty minutes, or for fifteen if time presses, or one is of an impetuous temperament, in fresh and weaker hypo solution. When we take it out of this solution, we find it to our advantage to rinse off the negative in running water several times before we put it in the negative-box under the washing-barrel. And we repeat the operation when we take it out. We also dry the little globules that delight to collect on glass. We dry them on the glass side of the plate, with a rag, and we dry them on the negative side, with a half-inch camel's-hair brush in the first place, and with absorbent cotton later.

Then we place a negative that has been trained in the way it should go, and ought to know how to demean itself properly, in the printing frame, upon the rack to dry.

64

The Negative, its Mark

I would not have it understood that we always take all these precautions; but we ought to take them, if we don't, and we are never sorry when we do.

The next thing that all the books advise is to varnish the negative. And I can speak of our varnishing method with a confidence the reader will rarely, if ever again, find on these pages.

Many and many a negative that might (as a print) have helped to make home happy, has been hopelessly lost by negligent or mistaken or over-indulgent varnishing. We shivered together as, in a low, awestruck voice, Jane read the directions for varnishing.

" 'Take hold of the plate, which has previously been made perfectly clean' (he speaks as if to scrub a gelatine film were the easiest thing in the world), 'and holding it as level as possible, pour quite deliberately, without stopping and with a firm, true hand, as quickly as possible, a small pool of the varnish. Lower, in turn, each of the four corners of the plate, thus imparting a kind of undulatory motion. Flow the varnish evenly entirely over the plate. This is important. Then pour back the surplus varnish into the bottle, but do not keep the plate motionless while the varnish is being drained off; give it a slow, rocking motion to prevent the formation of ridges. All should be done deliberately, but not so slowly that the varnish has time to dry. It should never fall on the plate in drops, but in an even and all the time undulating stream. Do not allow a particle of dust to strike the varnish before it is dry.'

"And here," Jane added, taking up one of our trustiest guides, "here is what Wilson says about it: 'By any convenient method heat the negative'—heat when the weather is almost enough to peel the films off the plate"—this was before we used our improved hypo bath—"heat 'until the hand can be borne upon it without pain.' Then he does like the other man. But listen to what Mr. England does: 'The method I have adopted for some time past is simple, efficient, and reliable. . . . It is to flood the negative, in the first place with dilute amber varnish, and when dry to coat it with ordinary hard spirit varnish.' Two times of that risky proceeding! It seems to me varnishing is the hardest of all!"

"Me too!" said the partner, dismally.

"Wilson says: 'All the labor and all the art thus far expended upon the negative may be sacrificed by heedlessness in varnishing.'"

"In our case it undoubtedly would be," said I.

"He says some varnishes require heat both for their application and for their drying; and heat is so hard to manage. And it will have to dry without any dust and be heated at the same time. We should have to shut it up in the chest with a spirit lamp, and the whole thing might take fire—it *could!*"

The Negative, its Mark

"Might, could, and would!" said I.

"It almost seems too dangerous to try," said Jane.

"Quite too dangerous," said I.

"What do you reckon would happen if we didn't varnish?" said she.

"I don't know; let us try and find out," said I.

We did try, and we did find out. We have never varnished a negative, and the only negative ever injured, whose injuries we can in anywise lay to its unvarnished truth, is one that I myself spoiled in retouching. It may be urged that had that negative been varnished the varnish could have been removed from the spoiled part and we could begin over again; but when I consider the kind of mess I should infallibly make removing the varnish, I am not so sure.

We fearlessly recommend to any amateur either beginning or pursuing the study, to let varnish alone. If he fancies that I exaggerate the difficulty of varnishing, there is nothing like trying a little pool of varnish on a spoiled negative, with his old clothes on, in a place where some varnish on the floor is not objectionable.

I have said that we did not long work in darkness with our developing. But it was not until about two years ago that we found Dr. Higgins's remarkable white light process; and as none of the professional photographers that we have visited in the East or the West, not even the superior boy in Boston, seem to have made trial of it, our experience may be of use.

It was in the " Photographic Annual " for 1890 that we first saw the account of Dr. Higgins's discoveries. The wagon and six oxen had toiled through the swamp to the railway station to bring us an anxiously expected photograph box. The " Annual " was in the box, and one of us fell upon it at once. She read the description aloud.

" Let us try one this evening," cried the reckless experimenter of the firm.

" We haven't any oxalate developer made up," said the restraining influence, " and it particularly says we need that."

" I don't think there is any difference in the light-defying powers of developers," was the easy answer; " anyhow, let us try with eikonogen, we have plenty of that made up. If it shouldn't work, we can try with the iron; we don't care much for those mill negatives that we have taken to-day, anyhow."

Not deigning any direct answer, the better influence read aloud impressively: " ' And what is the nature of this light-defying mixture? we hear you say. On the word of our generous friend, it is nothing but that well-known mixture of bromide and iron and potash, known as the ferrous oxalate developer—a developer yielding the very finest of negatives, staining neither the hands nor plate.' "

"THE WAGON AND SIX OXEN HAD TOILED THROUGH THE SWAMP."

She added, " It was done by the iron developer and gaslight."

" Very well," replied the cheerful rash one, " it will be done to-night by the eikonogen developer and a kerosene lamp."

" Do you want to follow the directions at all? Or will you just plunge into white light development? "

" I shall follow the directions implicitly, Jane, except as to the iron developer. The way I look at it is, that the plate must lose sensitiveness after the development begins, and that is the secret. If I am right, any developer will do as well as any other. If I am wrong, tell me how ever do we manage to develop our negatives in the daylight, with the light seeping into our dark room the way it does? "

Jane has a candid, reasonable soul; she could not gainsay the last argument. " Well, I don't care much if we do spoil these negatives," said she, pleasantly ; " I'll tell Jim to pump the barrel full."

" But isn't there something that must be done to the plates beforehand? " said Madonna, anxiously—she was as much interested in our new toy as we; " don't they have to be put into the plate-holder in ' total darkness ' ? "

" They were put in that way," said Jane ; " we read an article about plates being fogged before they were exposed, by the red light, and we determined to put ours in without any light. I think one or two of them got wrong side out; but it will not matter, they will fog just as readily with the white light, or they will show they haven't fogged."

That night, as the gibbous moon filled our east veranda with unearthly radiance, three dark figures crossed its lambent glow and disappeared in the shadows of an open door. Without, the wind soughed through the leafless trees; within, Jane had difficulty with a lamp-wick, and said she somehow felt sure the experiment wouldn't succeed. The three scientists were alone, our black retainers having taken the gibbous moon to light them on their way to a "festival."

Jane prepared a tray with enough developer (a feeble solution of eikonogen) to cover a negative and give no chance of a huge spot out in the air. The negative was removed from the slide and slipped into this tray in absolute darkness by one who shall be nameless. Before putting the plate into the tray it was brushed as usual; after it was in the tray the operator rubbed it over with her finger, which is something she always does, to break it gently to a negative that it is now in the developer and can't get out and may as well behave. A black cover was placed on the tray. The lamp was lighted. Jane read from the book the account of Dr. Higgins's success. "'Let the plate remain for two or three minutes,'" she read.

" It is almost five!" cried Madonna; "somebody look! I am really growing excited."

" Five minutes by the clock," said I.

Jane read: "'You can now lift the cover and examine with a fairly strong white light; one that is all that you desire for the purpose.'"

",I am going to look," said the discourager of hesitancy, boldly.

" It will be plumb spoiled, I reckon," said Jane—in the sacred privacy of home we allow ourselves the use of the dialect of the country.

It was a thrilling moment. No less than three distinct thrills chased each other down my spine, as I lifted the cover.

" Is it a blooming negative?" said Jane, with a slightly caustic accent.

" Is it fogged?" said Madonna.

" Neither," I answered firmly, "it hasn't started; developer can't be strong enough."

Jane suggested that perhaps that was the way that white light acted—wiped out the negative.

We increased the strength of the solution and added a trace of alkali. The developer now contained a solution which had half the strength of the normal developer in eikonogen and a touch of alkali.

We hazarded another plate in a solution of the same strength. Another five minutes passed; no mark on

71

—

the last white plate. We increased the strength of the developer, putting a nearly normal developer in the tray but not touching the first tray. In two or three minutes we looked at our later speculation, and the spectator uttered an exclamation of dismay; it was palpably fogged. Jane was so considerate that she did not remind me that the original experiment was with iron developer; she said maybe the solution was too strong. Then we examined the other negative, one that had been over-exposed, and with which, therefore, we had not dared to be very vigorous; lo! it was coming out, delicately, strongly, without a hint of fog.

"It *must* have been the developer!" said Madonna, with a sigh of relief.

We finished the development without further arrests to our hopes. We examined the negative freely, painted it in the deep shadow, held it in front of the kerosene lamp when necessary, and, in fine, treated it precisely as we should have treated it by the usual non-actinic photographic light. It was not injured in the least. We have since then developed many white-light negatives. We have tried pyro, eikonogen, hydro-quinone, eiko-hydro, and pyrocatechin. They appear to work with equal facility and security. The kitchen interior, on a former page, is a white-light negative. It was taken on a Carbutt Eclipse plate, the most sensitive of the Carbutt plates. We have developed in-

72

WEIGHING THE COTTON.

(Instantaneous white light negative.)

The Negative, its Mark

stantaneous exposures and orthochromatic plates by the
same method and with the same results. With at least
five developers, pyro, eiko, hydro, pyrocatechin, ferrous
oxalate, and mixtures of the different developers named,
you may safely trust your most sensitive plates, to our
certain knowledge. We habitually work by an orange
light, that is almost equivalent to white light, and quite
its equal in illuminating power.*

* As the reader may be interested to have Dr. Higgins's word for
his own experiments, and may not have the "Photographic Times
Almanac" at hand, I give his description : " For at least five years,
during which time I have developed up to even thousands of
negatives, I have pursued the course here given, making use of
neither dark-room nor non-actinic light of any kind. The plates
used have been the most sensitive attainable, and the exposures
both instantaneous and timed, and to have a foggy plate is something I have never known. Such results demand, of course, that
the plate be uninjured up to the time of development, and to
secure this, absolute perfection of camera and plate-holders is
one of the requisites. This each individual must personally see
to himself, taking, as in my advice to the 'Noviltiate' in your pre-
ceding 'Annual,' 'nothing for granted.' Next, the opening of the
plate-boxes, the insertion of the plates into the holders and their
removal therefrom for immersion in the developer, must be in darkness—total darkness.

"The plate now having seen (the word, I presume, is pardonable)
no light, except that incident upon exposure to view or object, can
only fog from having been so sent out by the manufacturer—a very
rare occurrence—or from the development. In the latter case, the
cause is either in the composition of the developer, or from the light

73

An Adventure in Photography

Our next developing sensation was orthochromatic
plates, of which we spoiled about a box before we
secured any freedom of action with them. I truly wish
I knew why we spoiled so many; but I don't, any more
than I know why they do not give us the slightest
trouble now. For a year we have been using Carbutt's
orthochromatic plates, and we have no more bother in
manipulating them than in manipulating their sup-
posed-to-be-hardier brothers. I think our first make

made use of in the development. Make certain, therefore, *ab initio*,
that your developer is all that can be asked of it, and then, having
filled out into your developing tray such quantity as will be sufficient
to cover your plate one-eighth of an inch deep, neither more nor less
(for this there are good reasons), remove your plate from the holder
and slide it into the developer, giving at once several rocking
motions to the tray to insure wetting the film evenly over its entire
surface, and the removal of air-bubbles, and cover over the tray.
So far in absolute darkness, and let the plate remain for two or
three minutes. You can now lift the cover and examine with a
fairly strong white light, one that is all that you desire for the
purpose. Re-cover for, say, five minutes or more (a normal exposure will average about fifteen minutes for ferrous oxalate
development), *pro re nata*, and re-examine, using any amount of
light, until satisfied that the development is finished.

"An instantaneous or insufficient exposure will require considerably more time than one that has been normal, as also will each
succeeding plate in the same developing solution. By this method
your negative is a creation of your own personal skill and judgment, and not of chance (*i.e.*, as far as the matter of development
goes), for it is of '*the things that are seen and not of the unseen.*'"

74

was not Carbutt's, but I am not disposed to shift the blame of our failure on that unremembered plate manufacturer's shoulders. I am inclined to think we overexposed them, and then, in an effort to secure density, used too strong a solution of eikonogen, and so secured only red fog. Red fog we certainly did obtain in large quantities. Orthochromatic plates may not do all that enthusiasts claim for them, but they certainly give admirable half-tints. They are particularly satisfactory in portraits, and they do good work in interiors.

We tried the celluloid films; but we shall stick to glass. The celluloid film is easily developed, but it curls and must be smoothed out with glycerine (which is a small matter, but a nuisance all the same), and we were obliged to print it under an immaculate plate of glass (it takes time to make a plate of glass immaculate), and one entire box of films, having been exposed to the damp, broke out in a perfect smallpox of pinholes; at least the pinholes came, and our sentiments of esteem and admiration for a gifted plate-maker, cause us to ascribe them to the damp. We do not know what damp, or how or when.

The beginner is always advised to stick to one make of plates. Does he ever follow the advice? We didn't; we wandered through the advertising lists from C to S. We tried the Cramer and the Carbutt, the Eagle and the Harvard and the Seeds. For brilliancy, we have

75

found the Carbutt unequalled, but equally superior in half-tones and softness are the Seed plates. For a beginner, I should unqualifiedly praise the Carbutt B. It gives more leeway for the photographer to make a fool of himself than any plate in the market. He can hit the right exposure more nearly on that long-suffering plate than on any slow plate I know, simply because two or three seconds seem to make little difference to its patience. The Seeds Sens. 23 is a kindly creature, too, gentle and tolerant. But out of the gloom of a tragic experience we beg new photographers to avoid all the rapid plates, Seeds 26, Cramer's 50, and the Carbutt Eclipse! They are not food for photographic babes. The slow plates all tend to increase contrast. They give half-tints more generously, they are far less apt to go astray in development; the same skill will produce a better picture out of them than out of the others.

As for developers, we have found that it pays to use the formulæ of the emulsion makers. With every box of plates comes a printed guide to the best use of the plates. Quite a little library comes with the Carbutt, Eagle, or Eastman plates and paper. The Carbutt eiko-cum-hydro, two-solution developer is as neat, as satisfactory, and as convenient as a developer can be. Nevertheless we have sometimes fancied advantages in making up our own developers from the drugs. We had a season of adversity struggling to get distilled water; but we found a thriftless, effectual, Southern solution of the riddle. We make enough developer for the negatives on hand, use it once and are done with it. Indeed, we are of the opinion that unless one can have the most unblemished purity of materials and likewise a freshness as of the dawn, it is better to use as little old developer as possible. The first trials of a home-made developer and a developer from the manufacturer will show little difference; it is time that is the test.

At the beginning of our adventure we tried the time-honored pyro. It was slow, it was dirty, it fogged the plates if you dared to push it, and it would not work if it was not pushed! During the reign of pyro we spent the time that we could spare from the studio in scrubbing our hands!

Then came the blessing of the tyro, hydroquinone. Ungrateful should we be were we to refuse it praise, because in later life, when we could manage our fiery steeds of developers better, we found that it lacked the daintier virtues of eikonogen. For the beginner hydroquinone can be recommended with a clear conscience. It will enable him to make negatives with contrast if any mortal developer can. Eikonogen was my favorite, hydroquinone Jane's, until the happy thought struck us to follow an example given in the "Photographic Annual" by Burton (whose book on printing

77

has been our constant guide), and to mix the two
together, thus acquiring the density and contrast of
hydro and the unsurpassed detail of eikonogen.

We went back—Jane alone can tell why, it was none
of my doing—to pyro; and Jane mixed up about a
gallon of the stuff and developed two negatives. They
were not poor, neither were they particularly good;
they belonged to the great middle class. We developed
them with shaking hearts, for they were on the edge of
a fog the entire time. Jane could not summon courage
to venture again with the uncertain pyro. We did,
however, try a few by white light; being negatives
taken for experiment, and uninteresting in composition
(in order that we might not regret their fate if they were
spoiled), of course they were beautiful specimens of their
kind.

The new developer, pyrocatechin or brenz-catechin,
in some respects is the most desirable of all. It works
very quickly, and the negative prints even better than
a brown pyro negative. It seems to have no inclina-
tion to fog or stain under protracted development, and
needs very little alkali.

But we soon found it for our advantage to make our
choice with a developer and stick to it, finding its faults
and putting up with them, as wives say of their husbands, the best one may. Eikonogen and pyrocatechin
are particularly good with instantaneous pictures.

The Negative, its Mark

The shutter invariably fascinates the beginner. It fascinated us. In our simple-minded way we proceeded to fire our shutter at the most difficult actions. We stood with trusting hearts and a Waterbury lens that could not get beyond a hand-gallop at best, and tried to catch the boat as it steamed past us not a stone's throw away. The result was such as, I am informed by the publishers, "it is absolutely impossible to reproduce!"

Nothing at this time pleased us more than to be firing off our snap shutter at every passing object. It was profitable experience—for the dealers.

"I have about decided," said Jane, as she pensively examined a blue print of a horse with six spectral legs, and a man with a large number of arms, "I have about decided that our lens isn't rapid enough to get very near to the objects!"

I agreed cordially. Unless one have a very rapid lens and a shutter like the Iris Diaphragm, for instance, it is wise to give the instantaneous figures a good long start down the middle distance.

Instantaneous development has excited heated discussions. Shall we develop with a gentle developer, and slowly, or with concentrated developer? We tried both. Both have yielded fair negatives.

On the whole, we were soon content to try a slow development for our instantictics. We have most comfort out of those that we have started in a weak solu-

79

tion of alkali, and then developed slowly in two solutions, one of eikonogen and one of alkali, in two different trays, shifting our negative from one to the other ; both being weak solutions, warranted not to strain the tenderest constitution. But it is superfluous and bewildering to give any cast-iron directions ; every negative, especially every under-exposed negative, as the instantiety may be considered, requires individual humoring to draw out its best. You have the two problems, the under-exposure, which calls for alkali, and the sensitive plate, which fogs at any excess of alkali. And somehow you must reconcile the two. The only way we can compass to achieve a reconciliation, is to give the alkali in small doses and very gradually, thereby not alarming the sensitive emulsion. We are often an hour coaxing a negative of this class ; but sometimes one receives one's reward in the excellent result. And, owing to our developing several negatives at once, the time does not hang heavily on our hands. On the whole, therefore, we prefer the mild, persuasive method rather than the forcing of strong developer.

As some reader may have the curiosity to care to know our development formulæ, I append a few. The Seed and Carbutt and Cramer formulæ all come with the plates, and can be obtained by any purchaser. They are perfectly trustworthy. So are the made-up developers sold by the several firms named.

The Negative, its Mark

A good ferrous oxalate, a good eiko, and a good hydro developer are given below, also a gem of a pyro-catechin developer. I cannot reconcile it with my conscience to help any young amateur with nice, white hands and a trusting heart, to the using of pyro, by providing him with a plausible-sounding formula.

A TRUSTY EIKONOGEN DEVELOPER.

No. 1.

Sulphite of sodium (crystals)	3 ounces.
Hot water	45 ounces.

Thoroughly dissolve, then add :

Eikonogen,	1 ounce.

No. 2.

Carbonate sodium crystals	4 ounces.
(or carbonate of potassium, 1¼ ounce.)	
Water	15 ounces.

To develop take of

No. 1	3 ounces.
No. 2	1 ounce.

If more contrast is required, increase the amount of No. 1 ; if less, more of No. 2. The developer can be used repeatedly * by adding each time a little of each of fresh solutions Nos. 1 and 2, according to above proportions. For developing a number of negatives at once, take 9 ounces of No. 1 ; 3 ounces of No. 2, and water 12 ounces.

With this developer we never expect anything but a good negative. It works better, we find, with the potas-

* But we do not recommend using old developer. You are likely to obtain density at the expense of the purity of your shadows. And you may save a dime's worth of developer and ruin half a dozen of a dollar and a quarter plates.

An Adventure in Photography

sium than with the sodium. We start with a solution of half No. 1 solution and half water, and gradually make it alkaline.

A Good Eikonogen Developer.

"Chautauqua" Developer, with Eikonogen in two solutions.

A.—Eikonogen............................128 gr.
    Crystallized sulphite of sodium.......... 1 ounce.
    Dissolve in warm water................. 16 ounces.
B.—Crystallized carbonate of sodium......... 1½ ounce.
    Water................................. 10 ounces.

For normal exposures take 3 parts of A and 1 part of B. To promote intensity add a few drops of a 10 per cent. solution of bromide of potassium.

"Chautauqua" Developer with Eikonogen. (In one solution, for instantaneous work.)

    Eikonogen.............. ....120 gr.
    Crystallized sulphite of sodium........... 1½ ounce.

Dissolve in 8 ounces of hot water and add carbonate of potassium 120 grains.

For use dilute with an equal bulk of water, and add a few drops of a 10 per cent. solution of bromide of potassium.

Gen. Brown's Treasured Hydroquinone Developer.

No. 1.—Sulphite of soda (pure crystals) ....240 grains.
    Water .... 4 ounces.
    Dissolve, and add hydroquinone........ 60 grains.
No. 2.—Saturated solution of carbonate of soda.

Developer : No. 1, two drams ; No. 2, one dram ; water to make up to four ounces.

This developer was the joy of Jane for many months. As a *brilliant* developer it has no superior.

82

The Negative, its Mark

—— -

"CHAUTAUQUA" DEVELOPER, WITH HYDROQUINONE, FOR GELATINE
DRY PLATES.

A.—Hydroquinone........................120 grains.
Sulphite of sodium, granulated........... 1 ounce.
Meta-bisulphite of potassium. .... 30 grains.
Water............................... 16 ounces.
B.—Carbonate potassium .... 1½ ounce.
Water............................... 16 ounces.

FERROUS-OXALATE DEVELOPER FOR GELATINE DRY PLATES (DR.
EDER's).

A.—Neutral oxalate potassium..............200 Gm.
Distilled water........................800 C.c.
Acidulate with oxalic acid.
B.—Proto sulphate of iron, crystals........100 Gm.
Distilled water........................300 C.c.
Sulphuric acid......................... 5 minims.
C.—Bromide of potassium .... 10 Gm.
Distilled water........................100 C.c.
D.—Hyposulphite of sodium................ 2 Gm.
Distilled water........................200 C.c.

Mix immediately before use three volumes of A with one volume
of B, and develop. Restrain with a few drops of C.

For over-exposure take less of the iron solution and add gradually
in small portions as required. To give the negative body, use C.

PYRO-CATECHIN DEVELOPER.

SOLUTION 1.

Water.... .... 3 oz. 3 drams.
Pyro-catechin.......... ....15 grains.

SOLUTION 2.

Carbonate of potassium...... .... 1½ ounce.
Water................................ 16 ounces.

|This simplest of developers works like a charm.

An Adventure in Photography

PARAMIDOPHENOL DEVELOPER, OR, THE GIANT.

Water............................. ....1,000 C.c.
Sodium sulphite .... 120 grams.
Potassium carbonate .... 40 grams.
Paramidophenol .... 4 grams.

BURTON'S MIXED EIKO AND HYDRO DEVELOPER.

Hydroquinone................................... 4 parts.
Sulphite of soda............... .... 12 parts.
A saturated solution of eikonogen in 10 per cent.
   sulphite of soda.................... .... 200 parts.
Carbonate of soda (in crystals) .... 25 parts.
Water up to............................. ...1000 parts.

DR. HIGGINS'S IDOL, OR, GEN. BROWN'S IMPROVED FERROUS OXALATE.

Ferrous sulphate............................ 8 ounces.
Water (hot)................................ 16 ounces.
Dissolve and filter ; when cool, add
   Tartaric acid................................ 5 drams.

The commercial " copperas," or " green vitriol " even, may be used if we select clear crystals. It may be prepared by the gallon, if necessary, and if *kept in the light* and *exposed occasionally to the sunshine*, it will always remain a clear, bright-green, limpid liquid.

Thus prepared, and added to the neutral oxalate stock solution as usually directed (though by cautious additions much more iron may be added without a precipitate), it will give you a developer infinitely better suited to the gelatine plate than the alkaline pyro in any form, and only equalled, according to my competitive experiments, by a properly prepared hydroquinone developer, which it far excels in rapidity.

But, as I have said, our favorite among the older developers is a "mixtery," as the old negro cooks would say, of eiko and hydro, prepared according to Carbutt's Eiko-cum-hydro formula, which goes with all his plates.

84

The Negative, its Mark

We use, also, his fixing bath, which is almost identical with the bath given below, as the reader may see for himself by comparing them.

English Measures—Troy Weight.	Metric Weights and Measures.
1 quart Water................................	1 litre.
4 ounces Sulphite of sodium crystals........ ..	120 grams.
After being dissolved add	
½ ounce Sulphuric acid.......................	15 c.c.m.
3 ounces Chrome alum, powdered..............	90 grams.
Dissolve and pour this into a solution of	
2 pounds Hyposulphite of soda................	1 kilo.
3 quarts Water............................ ...	3 litre.

This bath combines the following advantages : it remains clear after frequent use : it does not discolor the negatives, and forms no precipitate upon them. It also hardens the gelatine to such a degree that the negatives can be washed in warm water, provided they have been left in the bath a sufficient time. The plate should be allowed to remain in the bath five to ten minutes after the bromide of silver appears to have been dissolved. The permanency of the negative and freedom from stain, as well as the hardening of the film, depends upon this. Wooden boxes, with grooves to hold a number of plates, will be found both convenient and economical for fixing. When the bath becomes weakened by constant use, it should be replaced by a fresh solution.

CARBUTT'S NEW ACID FIXING AND CLEARING BATH.

Hyposulphite of sodium	16 ounces.
Sulphite of sodium crystals.................	2 ounces.
Sulphuric acid...........................	1 fluid dram.
Chrome alum............................	1 ounce.
Warm water.............................	64 ounces.

Dissolve the hyposulphite of sodium in 48 ounces of water, the sulphite of sodium in 6 ounces of water; mix the sulphuric acid with 2 ounces of water, and pour slowly into the sulphite sodium solution, and add to the hyposulphite; then dissolve the chrome alum in 8

An Adventure in Photography

ounces of water, and add to the bulk of solution, and the bath is
ready. This fixing bath will not discolor until after long usage, and
both clears up the shadows of the negative and hardens the film at
the same time.

Let remain two or three minutes after negative is cleared of all
appearance of silver bromide. Then wash in running water for not
less than half an hour, to free from any trace of hypo solution. Swab
the surface with a wad of cotton, rinse, and place in rack to dry spon-
taneously.

And here are three good reducing formulæ :

BELITSKI'S ACID FERRI-OXALATE REDUCER FOR GELATINE PLATES.

Water............................. .... 7 ounces.
Potassium ferric oxalate......... .... 2¼ drams.
Crystallized neutral sulphite of sodium......... 2 drams.
Powdered oxalic acid, from.............30 to 45 gr.
Hyposulphite of soda........... .... 1½ ounce.

The solution must be made in this order, filtered, and be kept in
tightly closed bottles; and as under the influence of light the ferric
salt is reduced to ferrous, the preparation must be kept in subdued
light.

REDUCER FOR GELATINE DRY PLATE NEGATIVES (FARMER'S).

Sat. sol. of ferricyanide of potassium........... ... 1 part.
Hyposulphite of sodium solution, 1 in 10...... ...10 parts.

REDUCER FOR GELATINE DRY PLATES.

Perchloride of iron........................... ...30 gr.
Citric acid.......................................60 gr.
Water.. ... 1 pint.

We do not believe in intensifying, but if you must
intensify this formula will hurt your negative as little
as any.

The Negative, its Mark

INTENSIFIER FOR GELATINE DRY PLATES WITH MERCURIC CHLORIDE AND HYDROQUINONE (DR. MALLMAN).

After whitening in the saturated solution of mercuric chloride, as usual, treat with an old hydroquinone developer ; the result is a bluish-black intensification, which is applicable to positives as well as negatives.

It is a ticklish matter cleansing a negative from stains, but here is a formula as safe as any :

CLEANING BATHS.—Solutions used to cleanse and clean a negative or positive of any kind from stains of development. The following have been found useful with different brands of plates: alum, 1 oz. ; water, 15 oz. ; citric acid, ¼ oz. ; water, 36 oz. ; chrome alum, ½ oz. ; citric acid, ¼ oz. Used after development. Wash off and immerse for three to five minutes. Wash and clear (fix): alum, 1 oz. ; citric acid, 1 oz. ; protosulphate of iron, 3 oz. ; water, 20 oz, ; should be freshly mixed. Saturated solution of alum, 20 oz. ; hydrochloric acid (commercial), 1 oz. Immerse the negative after clearing (fixing), having previously washed it for two or three minutes under the tap. Wash well after removal from alum and acid. This bath will act very kindly with dry negatives that have become discolored.

Finally, when all is over, and you gaze on the wreck of your hopes, in gelatine, here is a recipe for cleaning off your glass!

CLEANING OLD NEGATIVES.—Dissolve several ounces of common washing soda in two gallons of hot water. In this put the plates and leave them for twenty-four hours. At the end of this time many of the films will have disappeared. Those still adhering can be easily removed by using an old tooth-brush. After they are denuded of the old films put them in hot water, to which add a small quantity of hydrochloric acid; let them soak for an hour, and transfer them to pure hot water for another hour, after which they will be clean, and can be placed on edge to drain and dry.

CHAPTER V

THE pundits have a continually recurring phrase,
" Don't wobble! Stick to one thing; one plate, one
developer, one paper!" But, speaking now as one of
the ignorant, how, O wise ones, are we to know which
is the best plate, the best developer, the best paper, unless we do wobble? There are people who would make
photographic choice as irrevocable as marriage, without
permitting the privilege of courtship. I confess we
rambled too much. We were messing with half a dozen
kinds of paper at the same time. I would suggest a
compromise. Let the amateur, as a concession to his
light nature, be allowed a paper a season.

We would recommend him to begin on blue paper.
It requires no fussy toning and fixing; it prints out in
the frame, not like a ghostly platinotype, but distinctly;
he does not risk everything on a single act of judgment,
as in bromide printing, but may watch the process
throughout; and lastly, the washing is much simpler

'and easier than the washing of most other kinds of paper. Its one grievous fault is that it deteriorates with age.

Our first paper was an aged sample that had lost courage waiting for a customer. It had no longer any white tints, a faded light blue was its utmost effort at brightness. We supposed that was the way the paper always acted. We wondered that the formulæ could talk of white lights. But one day there came a paper fresh from the shop, and our eyes were dazzled by ravishing china-blue tints and pearly white.

How we struggled to get more of that paper! The "Queen," I think, was its name, and it came from Philadelphia, a city that I have always loved, because of its solid virtues, its magnificent charities, its well-descended people, and its adorable things to eat! Again and again did we beg our dealers to send us more of the "Queen;" instead, we received all kinds of paper with fine names, but never the "Queen." We often pondered on the problem. Had the manufacturer failed? Was his paper too good to sell, and had he been obliged to leave the business? Was he crushed by jealous rivals? Had the dealers been persuaded to boycott his superior wares?

We never found out; it remains a darksome riddle, like "Who was the Man in the Iron Mask?" We only know we never found the paper's like again. But we supplied its place in a less expensive way. Mr. Beach, in the "Amateur Photographer," recommended the manufacture of blue paper. We followed his advice, and found that blue paper is a very easy thing to make, and that the fresh article is infinitely superior to the stale. Where one can get it fresh daily from the manufacturer it is hardly worth while to take the trouble of preparing it, but where one must take the chances of its age, it is well worth the effort. We give the formula that we use at the end of this chapter. We apply the iron salts with a camel's-hair brush, flat and broad, brushing the paper lengthwise and then at right angles, leaving as few brush marks as we conveniently may—though, truth to tell, we never could find a trace of them in the printed page; the only mistake that was always brutally plain, was skipping the least portion of the paper in the brushing. We print until the shadows begin to look bronzed, then we take the paper out of the printing-frame and place it face downward in a washing-box. We let it stay some ten or fifteen minutes, then remove it to a fresh bath, still face downward. From this stage there is only a step to the last baths, where it can show its face and float about in company with its mates. We like to wash blue prints an hour or more. We fancy that thorough washing cannot be done in less time, and that we thus get a brilliant print. A brilliant print we certainly are able to get from

A COUNTRY ROAD,

(White lignt negative. See p. 72.)

—

moderate negatives. Very strong negatives are likely
to be harsh in blue prints, and very weak negatives will
be flat. The blue print does not give as much detail as
the albumen or the gelatino-chloride papers, but it gives
as much as any mat surface, unless it be possibly the
platinotype. It is urged against the blue print that it
has a disagreeable, sunken aspect. But has it, with
a fresh paper? We trow not. However, there is a
remedy in rubbing the blue print with encaustic paste.
I append our formula. The only danger is that unless
one is careful the paper may give a sudden lurch and
crumple under the hand. This happens when the paste
is rubbed on too lavishly, or when it dries unevenly.
When it happens, the only cure is to soak the print in
water, dry it, and start afresh.

We were not satisfied with our blue prints, of course.
We plunged recklessly into albumen paper. We made
a little fuming-box with tapes strung across, and a saucer
in the bottom for the ammonia, and we bought some
ready-made toning fluid, which toned with maddening
slowness, so that we could only get a streaked, reddish-
brown, do what we would, for our color. The paper
was too old, we afterwards discovered.

After experimenting with divers toning baths, we
have concluded that it does not matter so much whether
one choose bicarbonate of soda, tungstate of soda, or
something else; the great point is to wash off the free

nitrate of silver after the prints come out of the frame, and before they are toned, and to tone only one at a time. Of course, the books tell you that the skilful toning operator can tone twenty; and I have seen my friends, Mr. Hostetler and Mr. Hubinger, of Davenport, Iowa, toning what seemed to me an unlimited quantity with all the ease in the world; but *they* are skilful operators, we are not, and we prefer to take more time and not throw away so many prints—the floor of our studio, of a printing afternoon, is disgraceful enough to view as it is. A dozen is none too many to wash or to fix at a time, but we think that we have witnessed a distinct advance to unity of tone in our formerly allochroic prints since we gave them individual treatment. We fix twice; the first time in a moderately strong bath, the next and last time in a very weak one. How strong and how weak the inquiring photographer may see by our formulæ.

Temperature plays its part in printing as well as developing, and a change of temperature between the developer and the fixing bath, or a change between the toning bath and the fixing bath, will have almost equally bad effects. Of course you may escape; there are inscrutable decrees of nature that protect folly, and fall with a dull, sickening thump on wiser heads; they may see you through in safety! And you may play whist and, out of sheer idiotic greed, lead for the first

lead the sneak that is the only chance to save the odd
trick! I don't know why these trials to faith are permitted; I only know that they are. But you need not
fancy that they will go on; by chance you have hit
upon some loophole in photographic law and crawled
through, without knowing; but you cannot count on
hitting it, again!

A second fixing bath we have come to regard as essen-
tial to the security and permanence of the prints. We
may be wrong, but as a second bath is so little trouble,
and may be so helpful, why not use it?

Our method in printing has brought us good results,
and it may be acceptable to some amateur; while, if it
shall not seem so good as his own, he will have the
pleasant sensation of superiority, and no harm will be
done in either case.

After printing—we print according to the good old
rule, Print until all detail is out strong and bold and
sharp, in the high lights, and the shadows are bronzed
—we remove the print from the frame and place it
in a washing-box filled with tepid water (in summer the
water is tepid enough of itself, without heating), and
there we let the print remain for five or ten minutes.
We have several prints in at a time, and shift them in
order to give each the same chance to wash and be clean.

Now, we pour off the water, and let them soak in
clean water a few minutes more. This is repeated once

or twice more, making in all, four or five changes of water before they go into washing-box No. 2, which is filled with a weak acid solution (to one gallon of water one ounce of acetic acid, or, if you are bold and daring, to one trayful of water a few drops of the acid), where they are completely immersed, one by one. Keep them constantly in motion in this bath. They stay about ten minutes, according to the best authorities. Then we wash them again in several changes of water. It is thought desirable to be sure that all the acid is washed away before placing them into the toning bath ; but, myself, I cannot see why, in the case where acetic acid is used in the toning bath, there should be any danger in an additional minute whiff of it coming with the prints. However, Jane is faithful in following directions; she is more, she is obsequious ! And we wash the acid off, and Jane sniffs vigilantly until the last odor has departed.

The toning bath now comes on to the stage, in a clean porcelain tray. Wide is the range of toning fluids. To understand how wide, one must be a little wise in the mysteries of the process. Why do we wash, and why do we tone, and why do we fix? I have no objection to answering, because I can quote some one else, and shall not have to rummage among a rather shop-worn scientific stock, left over from my schooldays.

We wash to get rid of the nitrate of silver in the silver sensitized albumen paper. We try to get rid of it, because we don't want it to take up the valuable time of our gold. As to the part the gold plays in the business, here it is, clearly defined:

"A solution of chloride of gold. What can this do? Gold is what might be called an ascetic metal; it likes to live alone. In other words, it is easily reduced from its salts to the metallic state. So when this sheet of paper, covered all over with silver salts, is brought into a solution of chloride of gold, the silver having a great attraction naturally for chlorine and the gold parting willingly with its chlorine, it is no more than can be expected to find the chlorine leaving the gold and uniting with the silver, forming of course chloride of silver; the dark sub-chloride, when the silver has been reduced to the sub-chloride by the action of light, and the white chloride, when the silver is unaltered; and then, the gold, having lost that which held it in solution, has nothing to do but come down as a precipitate of metallic gold, and so metallic gold is deposited upon the picture." *

We use a bath rather weak in gold—at least, that is our principle; a liberal hand sometimes gets beyond our rule—preferring a slow and gradual toning. We tone by a weak white light, and we keep the print face up in the toning bath and well covered with the fluid.

The moment to take away the prints is the riddle of

* H. M. McIntyre, quoted in "Wilson's Photographics," p. 202.

the toning process. If you take them away before enough gold has been deposited you will have a raw, streaked picture, unfit even for the reckless hospitality of an amateur photographic album; a picture, moreover, doomed to an early fading. If, on the contrary, one tone too long, the prints will assume a sunken, ashen tint, and are then called "degraded." Most of our first season's printing was "degraded." Yet while it is so important to rescue the little dears before they become degraded, but not before they have taken all the gold they can absorb this side the degraded point, it is no more possible to direct the student infallibly to that moment of fate than it is to tell a cook just when she is to take the risen dough out of the bowl. In both cases the operator must have a trained eye, and the amateur can only train his eye by spoiling a few—or a great many—prints.

There are all shades and several colors of toning effects. You always have to allow for the bleaching of the hypo, and therefore to tone several shades deeper in tint than you wish the eventual result to be. It is a useful plan to test the toning bath for any subtle thief of an acid reaction that may have crept in. Litmus paper is always a good creature in a studio, and you can get enough to last a year, for a quarter.

Some printers put the prints that have been toned, in an acid bath (three to five grammes of pure muriatic

acid to a litre of water) before putting them into the
hypo; others merely wash them a single time and put
them in the hypo. We have always thought that we
had enough of a circus in our printing process without
the muriatic acid act; nor are we aware that we have
been punished for slighting it.

At first, to obtain different colors in toning (for
naturally we hankered to get every tint of which we
had ever heard or read), we used to follow Burton's very
complete and intelligible directions. If we wanted a
"warm tone," we soaked the print in salt and water; if
we desired a purple, in carbonate of soda and water.
But we soon agreed with our author that certain brands
will give naturally one tint and certain other brands the
other tint. In our efforts to get the purple tints which
at one time we craved on ready sensitized paper, we
only succeeded in getting a mongrel bluish-brown,
which Mr. Burton aptly characterizes as a "color quite
indescribable but certainly far from agreeable." And
we came to his sensible conclusion that such a brand
was "not suitable for toning, other than to a brown."
We also picked up a belief that certain toning baths
should be used with certain toning papers; for instance,
that we were not required to use a purple toning bath
with a paper of brown tendencies.

The temperature of the toning bath should be barely
tepid. In warm weather the water is likely to attend to

that, itself. Some of the wise advise a temperature of ninety degrees for all the solutions; but Burton never allows his thermometer to show more than seventy degrees. I think we must have had about everything in the way of temperature, and certainly sometimes we were warmer than seventy-five, and still were not injured.

The washed prints are now fixed for twenty to twenty-five minutes in hypo. If hypo be not alkaline—and it has the usual perversity of photographic materials and loves to outwit the painstaking amateur by a sly acid turn—the prints may fade; therefore it is important to make the bath alkaline. Ammonia is simple, and has the advantage of telling when it is present in sufficient quantities. As soon as the operator perceives the odor he can stop adding alkali.

We like to give each print as it is placed in the fixing bath a good wash of the hypo. We put it in and then press it under, face downward. As soon as all the prints are in, we take the lowest print out and put it on top, and so on through the company. Burton advises repeating this four times.

He advises the secondary bath of weak hypo, which we came to find valuable; and he would not use a stronger proportion of hypo than two ounces to a pint of water. He would have a large quantity of the bath. He has his ample bath from principle; we had it because it makes up more quickly and easily with the larger measures.

After the fixing comes the washing. Newton has "a simple and effectual method of cleaning the prints of hyposulphite of soda by employing the acetate or nitrate of lead." He says that it does not impair the permanence of the prints. Myself, I cannot help feeling that for the amateur it should not much condemn a method if it do "impair the permanence of prints," for so few of our prints are really demanding indestructibility, and so many would better quietly slip out of existence. Where is the sister or brother of the guild that has not, during his callow stage of satisfaction, given his kindred and friends prints that they are now displaying heedlessly as his or her work, while the giver wishes them in the fire?

The proper way to wash prints, when running water is not obtainable, is to keep them in motion, and shift from one tray to another, "using a clothes wringer frequently between operations."[*] This is to be kept up for "three or four hours"[†]—or until the operator faints at the trays! The final act is to place each print "on a sheet of clean glass, first, face downwards, then face upwards, for a few minutes, while a stream of water plays on it."[‡] Warm water is best to use.

---

[*] "Wilson's Photographics," p. 208.
[†] Burton, "Photographic Printing," p. 54.　　　[‡] Ibid.

An Adventure in Photography

This, I repeat, is the way we doubtless ought to wash our prints; the simple, actual, unpretentious way that we do wash them is to put them in a huge washing-box that contains about four gallons of water, distributing the prints about as well as we can, so that they may be separated; and leave them to fight it out with the hypo' for a varying period, which depends on our other avocations. When we think of it, in half an hour, we go and hoist the huge box and pour out the gallons of water, and fill the box with fresh water and sozzle the prints about in it for a while. Another period of placid elimination, generally devoted on our part to the evening meal. We then pay a second visit to the prints, sometimes two, or, in particularly conscientious seasons, three or even four, and we generally—unless it is too late or we are too tired—wash the prints off on glass, in the manner recommended. I am inclined to think that our method will be popular with amateurs in the future, as I suspect some variation of it has been popular in the past. We have some four-year-olds trained in this way, and they show no signs of deterioration.

At one time we had a slight experience with plain paper. I salted and silvered some Saxe paper and printed on it. Imagine my surprise when I obtained some very pretty prints! In consequence, we are going to try plain paper in a rather more exhaustive fashion. We had so little difficulty—that is, the poorer photographer of the firm had, for she worked alone, because Jane was too busy with art embroidery to accompany and protect the experiment—in making tolerable prints from home-made paper, that it occurs to us that the case of plain paper and blue paper may be analogous: namely, that freshly made paper may make all the difference in the world in the results. It is hard to tell the best of my plain paper prints from a platinotype, except for the purplish tone. Very rich purple tones can be obtained, as well as many beautiful browns. The toning and fixing are no more difficult than albumen paper toning or fixing; indeed, are almost the same processes. And the prints themselves have a delicacy, a clearness, and at the same time a rich depth that are most attractive.

Plain paper is salted in a very quick and easy way; there is little chance to make mistakes. It is silvered as easily as blue paper is sensitized.

One day an awful thing happened to a whole batch of our prints. They were taking the treatment like lambs; they had shown rich red-brown in the toning bath. The whites were crystal clear, or, rather, they were of the translucent porcelain clearness so precious to the photographer. We immersed them in hypo, with a tranquil mind. Jane took out one and said: "Well, this is pleasant!"

Then I knew there had been a catastrophe; I knew it

as distinctly as when she held out the print before my gaze.

"Every one!" said she, in a tragic tone.

Our beautiful prints were mottled all over, and presented an extraordinary burnished appearance among the mottles.

"What should you call it?" says Jane.

"I should call it the measles, complicated by metallic spots," I answered. There was nothing to do with the prints but send them after a long line of crushed hopes. They went by the Black river road, like the others, and we read Burton and Wilson all the evening.

Another time the mottled effect appeared the instant the prints left the frame, which was considerate, sparing us the trouble of toning.

As measles are caused for the most part by the paper, the nearest remedy is to reproach the dealer and discard the paper. Sometimes, however, the hypo bath (when acid) is the mischief-maker, in which case the remedy is apparent. Mealy prints are more dispiriting than measly prints, because in the latter trouble one can always find some one else to blame, but mealiness belongs generally to the printer. It comes from printing on very weak negatives, from too little silver in the paper (when one makes plain paper prints this is common), from too much gold in the toning bath, or from too little, from using a toning bath too fresh, or

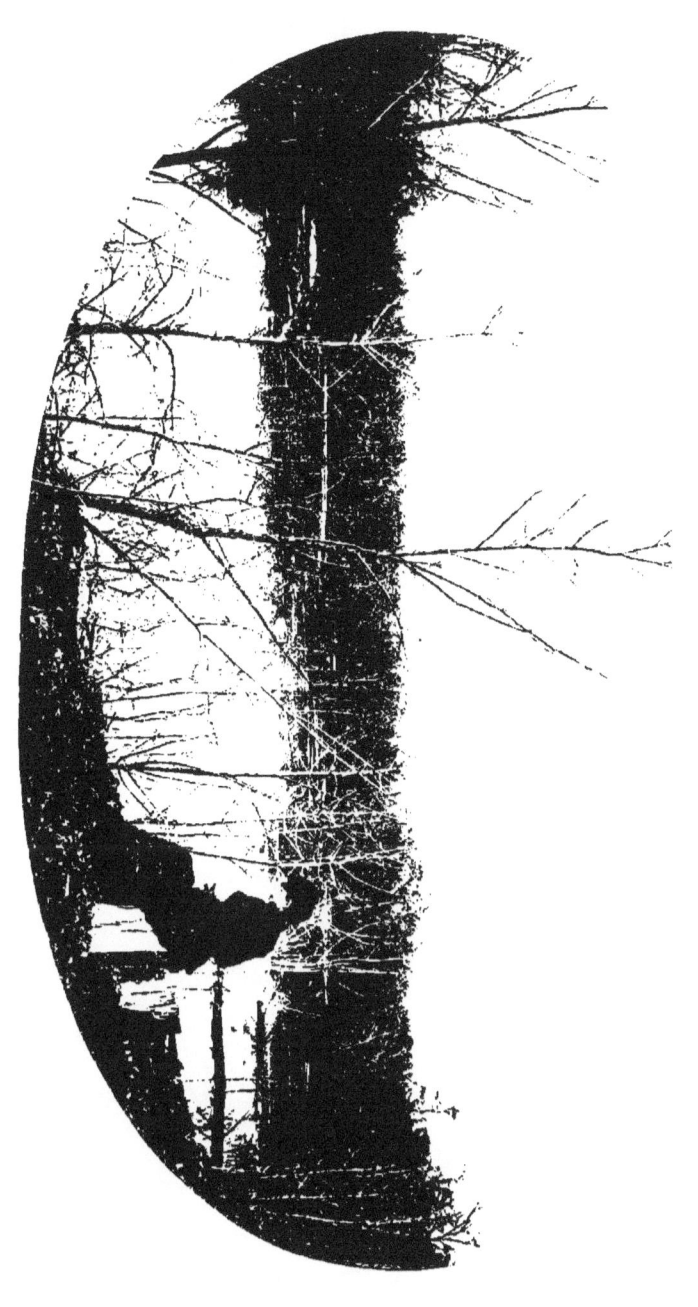

from washing the prints too long. Never was there a
trade that needed to have for its motto Josiah Allen's
Wife's great rule of conduct: "Be megum! Whatever
you do, be megum!" more or oftener than photography.
Wash enough, but don't wash too much. Tone enough,
but don't tone too much. Have the toning bath fresh,
but not too fresh. Make the hypo bath strong, but
not too strong. "Be bold! be bold! and evermore be
bold!" But be not *too* bold! On either side stands
ruin, grim and sure! Considering all the things that
can happen to an albumen print, the marvel is so many
tolerable ones appear all the time. Yellow patches and
stains are another terror. They come from the careless
manipulation of the paper, or from the least trace of
hypo on the fingers. The remedy is, Be Clean! They
have not bothered us much—not that we are especially
neat, but that our hypo arrangements are kept apart
from the other things, and we wash our hands every
time we go near the contaminating influence. Yellow-
ing of the paper may happen to the most careful printer,
but it happens persistently to the careless, who are too
lazy to make their hypo bath up fresh each time. It
happens also as a gentle call to time from any acid that
gets into the hypo bath. Warm weather will cause it,
or the keeping of paper too long.

Some of our prints used to go through all the processes with every promise of a fair future, and then

emerge from the fixing bath looking well enough by reflected light, but curdled and spotty and queer-looking by transmitted light.

Many a print did we throw aside as useless because of this—a needless waste of good prints that might have been saved by merely fixing them longer. Spotted prints are not fixed enough; "Prints," says Wilson, "should be left in the solution until you can see nothing but the fibre of the paper in the white parts of the print when held up to the light. If this is not done, they are apt to fade or turn yellow in a short time."

Sometimes the prints turn perverse and refuse to tone at all; ours were greatly addicted to this wicked habit; but the best remedy that we know is to " warm them."

Probably the most exasperating, most varied, and most frequent evil habit of the albumen paper is its tendency to *blister*.

And the thicker and richer the albumen coating, the greater the probability of blisters; because blisters come from the defective preparation of the albumen coats.

Nothing makes a print look more loathsome than blisters. The uneven action of the albumen may be caused by change of temperature in the different solutions. That is a common explanation, and my worst experience with blisters bears it out. I was using fresh paper, obtained from a photographer in town. It acted admirably in the toning bath, but the instant that it entered the hypo it blistered completely. There was not the space of a large pin-head free. I put one print into strong salt and water and for the next print I warmed the bath; both prints came out perfectly free from blisters.

Sixteen ounces of salt to one gallon of water is Wilson's formula.

Dr. Schnaus declares that an absolutely reliable preventative is to lay the sheet of paper, before printing, on blotting paper and to wash off the back with a wet sponge. The paper is then dried in the air, as drying by heat causes red spots.

We keep solutions at nearly the same temperature, and have had almost no trouble from blisters.

Arnold, in " The American Annual of Photography" for 1892, gives a simple but excellent formula, adding one ounce of alcohol to every ten ounces of toning bath.

And here are a few maxims from the same book, every one of which we know to be good.

A FEW REMEDIES AGAINST BLISTERING OF ALBUMEN PAPER.

Do not dry the paper by excessive heat.

Avoid acidity in solutions.

Moisten the print before washing with a sponge saturated in alcohol.

Immerse the print before fixing in weak alum solution.

Add a trace of aqua ammonia to the fixing bath.

An Adventure in Photography

Another, only a little less annoying, trick of albumen paper is to contract or to stretch in the printing frame. It invariably chooses the time for this caper when we are printing portraits, because it knows well that a land-scape may be broadened or lengthened and no great harm done, but if a face be flattened or elongated a hairsbreadth, the model of the picture will never forgive it. A photographic "wrinkle" to avoid such distortion is to moisten the sheet, pin it to a block, and dry the middle of the sheet first, driving the wrinkles into the edges. Our only device to amend our mistakes was to turn the paper about in such a way that round faces got the benefit of being lengthened, while we widened hatchet faces by placing the paper the opposite direction.

Perhaps, all things taken into account, it is not strange that the amateur seeks ever a new printing process. We read in Burton of the merits of paper coated with gelatine instead of albumen; glossy, like albumen, but more permanent, not so likely to be ruined by over-toning, doing as well by a thin negative as the bromide, yet giving a good picture from a "plucky" negative. We tried the "aristotype," the "chloride of silver," the "gelatino-chloride," the "emulsion" paper, all of which are as much alike as Betsy, Elizabeth, Bessy and Bess, who all went together to seek a bird's nest, and a bird's nest found with two eggs in it, and each took one, yet left one egg in it! The first paper that we received was called—but, no, I shall not give its name, the manufacturer may have repented and be leading a better life, making a paper that does not cause profanity over the length and breadth of this wide land; and I would not recall the irrevocable past. At the time, I must say, however, he didn't seem likely to repent; he had, in fact, what I should call a "cockiness" of spirit. He said in his circular that his brand of paper gave tones ("a *range* of tones") unapproached by any brand on the market (which was a tarradiddle, but no matter); he said that its softness, its richness, could hardly be described; he said that his combined fixing and toning bath was a marvel of rapidity (which it was *not*), and he said that possibly the paper might curl slightly before washing, but it only needed to be soaked and managed with a little care. That was what he said; this is what it did!

It went into a spasm the instant that it left the printing frame, curling up into the very tightest of spirals. It crawled and squirmed and twisted and wriggled and tried to roll itself up in the washing water, like a live creature! One needed three hands to manage it at all, two hands to hold the—the *beast*, and one to rock the tray!

After we managed, between us, to wash it without its tearing itself to pieces, it developed a new freak; of a sudden, it became the most fragile and slippery paper in the world, and as it still curled as playfully as at first, whenever we restrained it there would be a tear in the sheet. Before the bath was over it was rent in half a dozen places, but just as sprightly as ever. Oh, but we had a lively time! It went on curling and capering and rolling and rending until the end of the chapter, and to make the story short, we obtained exactly one decent print out of the package. And Jane declared, give her the honest albumen paper that knew when it had enough to drink and lay down quietly, instead of this insatiable rioter!

We succeeded better with a second package—by dint of extreme care; but we lost almost half our paper.

However, we were consoled for everything by the very next brand (the " Peerless ") that we tried, and the " Omega " was equally kind.

The best brands of the gelatine paper have their faults, but they are not unmanageable faults, and the manipulation is decidedly simpler than with albumen.

Its worst tendency is the delicacy of the gelatine coating, which requires careful handling until it is hardened in the alum bath; after that, it seems to be as tough as albumen, and may be handled freely. The washing is a degree less than the washing of albumen prints.

There have been a number of objections made to combining the toning and fixing operations, the point of them being that one has no security that a print is fixed simply because it is toned, and that to remove the print is to risk its becoming yellow or mealy, or likely to fade away. We have tried both the combined and the single baths, and confess our preference for the combined bath, because we can judge better as to the color of the print when we do not have to allow for reduction in hypo. We make our peace with our caution by afterwards fixing the print in a very weak hypo bath. There is very little change of color, this way. And I am gratified to learn that so high an authority as Burton approves of a combined bath, taking the same precaution. Aristotypes darken perceptibly after they are dried ; and allowance must be made for this fact.

The gelatine papers give a stronger print from a weak negative than the albumen; but they do not offset this advantage by giving too hard a print from a strong negative. A hard negative will make a hard print in albumen, and it will make a little harder print in gelatine, but a good plucky negative does not give a hard print on either paper.

The question of intensifying a negative by printing has always interested us. There is a very good reason ; we have had so many thin negatives. We have tried printing under tissue paper ; for we could, without the books, see that if we could contrive to print more slowly, contrast would be greater. Tissue paper gives a more vigorous picture, indeed, supplies all the vigor one is likely to ask ; but tissue paper—at least *our* tissue paper

An Adventure in Photography

—is an impressionist after Dr. Emerson's own heart;
and it returns to us, in the place of our thin, sharply cut
picture, abounding in the finest kind of detail, a fuzzy,
out-of-focus landscape, as broad as broad can be!

For obtaining contrast by printing, I know of nothing
better than printing under yellow glass. The detail is
preserved and contrast secured at the same time, for
which we may thank the non-actinic nature of yellow, I
presume. Printing in the shade is, I hardly need to say,
much slower than printing in the bright sunlight; and
therefore is "indicated" for thin negatives. But we
have found that printing in the shade, on a bright sunny
day, is better for the great bulk of negatives; indeed, for
all except the harsh negatives. Even in their case it is
a question whether it may not be better to sun the paper
before printing, and to print in the shade. Exposing
the paper for a few seconds only, has a magic effect on
the harshness of some negatives.

Speaking for ourselves, as two humble adventurers
who do not profess to be guides, we have found it less
troublesome to print according to paper, putting our
thin negatives on bromide paper, and our harsh negatives on platinotype. We do not, however, have many
hard negatives, because we reduce them. Thin negatives
print incomparably on the bromide papers; and it really
seems a waste of time to bribe other papers that do not
want them, to entertain them, with yellow glass and shade.

Printing

Vignetting, "printing in," masking, and the like, as well as combination printing, I defer to the chapter entitled Tricks, for they are to our mind all more or less artifices with which the photographer makes out a different story from the sun's real tale.

FORMULÆ.

To accommodate, at one and the same time, those who always skip formulæ and those who seek formulæ with an unslakable thirst, I have collected, in this retired spot, a few of the least risky.

1—To Sensitize Blue Paper for Cyanotypes.

A.—Citrate of iron and ammonium..............1¾ ounce.
Water.................................8 ounces.
B.—Ferricyanide of potassium.................1¼ ounce.
Water.................................8 ounces.

Mix equal parts immediately before use and float the paper, Rives plain, upon it for three minutes ; hang up to dry.

We find better results when we brush the solution on the paper instead of floating.

2—Burton's Plain Paper Emulsions.

No. 1.

A.—Nitrate of silver........................400 grains.
Water......................... 4 ounces.
B.—Gelatine (soft).......... .... 80 grains.
Chloride of ammonium........ .... 80 grains.
Citric acid............................ 120 grains.
Water................. .... 8 ounces.

An Adventure in Photography

No. 2.

A.—Nitrate of silver...........................400 grains.
    Water.................................... 4 ounces.
B.—Gelatine (soft)......................... 80 grains.
    Chloride of ammonium.................... 80 grains.
    Citric acid.............................120 grains.
    Carbonate of soda (dry).................. 45 grains.
    Water................................... 8 ounces.

No. 3.

A.—Nitrate of silver.........................400 grains.
    Water.................................... 4 ounces.
B.—Gelatine (soft)..... .... 80 grains.
    Chloride of ammonium.................... 80 grains.
    Citric acid. .... 60 grains.
    Carbonate of soda (dry).................. 80 grains.
    Water....................................... 8 ounces.

In my hands the first formula gives an emulsion suitable for preparing paper to be used for printing from dense negatives, the second from medium negatives, and the third from thin negatives.

Mr. Burton says that the "best way of coating is certainly by floating, allowing three to four minutes, but the quantity of the emulsion needed is considerable. It is possible to get an even coating by brushing with cotton wool in the following way : the paper is laid on a sheet of glass, or a clean board, and is thoroughly and evenly damped with the solution by brushing over the surface several times in directions at right angles. It is put on one side for ten minutes or a quarter of an hour, to get surface dry, when the operation is repeated. . . . I have never been able to get an even enough coating by brushing only once. The temperature of the operating-room should be about seventy degrees Fahrenheit, or else the emulsion should be warmed. The paper is best dried pretty quickly before a fire, or near a stove, after it has lain for about four or five minutes to get surface dry."

The longer the paper is printed the richer the tones, therefore strong negatives are usually preferred. But Mr. Burton, by his separate treatment for thin and dense negatives, gives good tones for all.

Mr. Burton prints on the platinum bath, Clark's Process :

Printing

CLARK'S PLATINUM BATH.

Dissolve sixty grains of chloro-platinite of potassium in two ounces of distilled water (if you cannot get distilled water, and we have found a great many things easier to get than it, take boiled water cooled, it does apparently just as well). This makes the stock solution. For the toning bath take

```
Stock solution .................................1 dram.
Nitric acid....  ........  ...................  ....3 drops.
Distilled water...............................3 ounces.
```

But the prints may be toned by gold. Here are some good baths:

```
Gold Toning.—Tungstate of soda.............20  grains.
               Phosphate of soda .............20  grains.
               Boiling water ...............  3  ounces.
Dissolve, and add
               Chloride of gold............... 1  grain.
Allow to cool, and add
               Water....................... 5  ounces.
               Chloride of gold..............15  grains.
               Water...  .................... 7½ ounces.
```

Two drams of this solution, neutralized with a pinch of chalk, are added to ten ounces of boiling water, and filtered into a quart bottle in which two drams of acetate of soda have been placed. When the soda is dissolved, the solution is made up to twenty ounces. The bath should be allowed to stand for some hours before it is used.

Generally, plain prints are washed in several changes of water before immersing them in the toning bath; but when he uses the platinum bath Mr. Burton puts paper coated with the first two emulsions directly into the toning bath. Paper coated with the third emulsion he washes off in a weak solution of citric acid to neutralize the alkaline character.

The color in the printing frames should be a rich brown with either of the first two formulas, a deep purple with the third.

The printing is very quick, whichever of the formulas be used, but with No. 3 it is extraordinarily so. Indeed, paper coated with emulsion prepared by this formula is, I think, more sensitive than that by any other printing-out process that I know of. It is so sensitive that it is quite necessary to take extra precautions in working it.

The paper keeps better than the general plain paper, and no mention is made of fuming. I know that I did not fume, and the prints took a rich purple very quickly. He makes the solutions in the following manner.

You will observe that each emulsion consists of two solutions.

" The two solutions are heated to a temperature of one hundred and ten degrees to one hundred and twenty degrees Fahrenheit. The temperature should not be greater than one hundred and twenty degrees, as there is a great chance that some of the insoluble silver salts produced will be thrown down in the granular form. A is then added slowly to B, with much stirring. The emulsion is filtered through a double thickness of cambric, and is then immediately ready for use. If it is wished to keep the emulsion for any length of time, ten per cent. of alcohol, in each ounce of which a few grains of thymol have been dissolved, should be added to the solution."

The platinum bath has what Mr. Burton calls "a good dose of salt," which I took to mean about half a teaspoonful.

It is a beautiful formula, and works like a charm.

114

Printing

SOME GOOD OLD STAND-BYS FOR ALBUMEN PAPER.

E. L. WILSON'S BATH.

Water	32 fluid ounces.
Acetate sodium	60 grains.
Chloride sodium	60 grains.
Chloride gold	4 grains.
Nitrate uranium	4 grains.

Neutralize the gold and uranium, previously dissolved in a little water, with sufficient bicarbonate soda. Before using, add gold to renew the bath, as necessary.

LIESEGANG'S COMBINED TONING BATH.

Water	32 ounces.
Hyposulphite of soda	8 ounces.
Sulpho-cyanide of ammonium	1 ounce.
Acetate of soda	½ ounce.
Saturated solution of alum	2 ounces.

and

Water	8 ounces.
Chloride of gold	15 grains.
Chloride of ammonium	30 grains.

Pour the gold solution into the hypo solution, then add thirty grains of freshly prepared chloride of silver.

THE CHAUTAUQUA TONING BATH.

Dissolve fifteen grains of chloride of gold and sodium in fifteen ounces of water. Take of this solution three ounces, pour it in the toning dish, test for acidity with litmus paper, and *neutralize* with bicarbonate of soda, and add thirty grains of acetate of soda and thirty ounces of water. Prepare the solution an hour before using it.

If warm tones are wanted, add a little acetic acid to the last washing water.

For this bath the sensitizing silver should be neutral, for which purpose a small portion of carbonate of silver should be kept in the silver stock bottle.

An Adventure in Photography

TONING BATH FOR READY SENSITIZED PAPER.

A.—Water.................................... 1 litre.
 Chloride of gold....................... .... 1 gram.
B.—Water................... .... 1 litre.
 Borax................................ ...10 grams.
 Tungstate of soda........................40 grams.

DR. LIESEGANG'S TONING BATH.—*With Tungstate of Soda.*

Boiling water................................. 1 litre.
Tungstate of soda............................20 grams.
Chloride of gold .... 1 gram.

Can be used immediately after cooling.

DR. LIESEGANG'S TONING BATH.—*With Phosphate of Soda.*

Water.. 1 litre.
Phosphate of soda........ ....15 grams.
Chloride of gold.............................. 1 gram.

DR. LIESEGANG'S TONING BATH.—*With Carbonate of Lime (Chalk).*

Water.................................... ... 1 litre.
Chloride of gold.... .... 1 gram.
Carbonate of soda............................15 grams.
Chalk.................... .... 5 grams.

After twelve hours the bath is perfectly clear and colorless, when it is ready for use. It is very durable, and gives fine tones.

A good hypo solution has been given, as a one-to-five solution assured of its alkaline character by ammonia, but here is a bicarbonate of soda fixing bath that has served us well.

HEARN'S FIXING BATH FOR ALBUMEN PRINTS.

Water.....................................8 ounces.
Sat. solution of hypo........... ....1 ounce.
Bicarbonate of soda in sat. solution............1¼ ounce.

116

Printing

The second hypo bath is only a one to fifteen or to ten solution.

A Full Formula for Aristotypes for those who Prefer Separate Toning.

The prints are first washed in one or two changes of water, and then toned in a mixture of the following toning baths:

Bath No. 1.

Distilled water	35 ounces.
Double crystallized acetate of soda	1¼ ounce.
Chloride of gold solution (strength, 1 grain to 1½ ounces of water)	3 ounce.

Bath No. 2.

Distilled water	35 ounces.
Sulpho-cyanide of ammonium	¾ ounce.
Chloride of gold solution (strength, 1 grain to 1½ ounces of water)	3 ounces.

The solutions are to be kept separate, and when ready for use may be mixed by adding 2¼ ounces of No. 2 to 7 ounces of No. 1. The bath as mixed will keep clear, and as it slows in toning, more of the gold solution can be added.

To judge of the right tone, the prints should be examined by looking through them, or by transmitted light. When it is obtained they are removed to fresh water, washed a minute or two, and placed in a fixing bath of

Water	1 ounce.
Hyposulphite soda	5 ounces.

The fixing is completed in one or two minutes, then the prints should be washed for an hour in frequent changes of water, and finally place them in an alum bath for about three minutes, made as follows:

Water	35 ounces.
Powdered alum	1¾ ounce.

They should now be washed in six or eight changes of water until

117

An Adventure in Photography

the milky color in the water disappears. They may then be washed for an hour or so, or left in the water over night.

LIESEGANG'S COMBINED TONING BATH.

Water.... ....32 ounces.
Hyposulphite of sodium........................ 8 ounces.
Sulphocyanate of ammonium.................. 1 ounce.
Acetate of sodium............. .... ½ ounce.
Saturated solution of alum................ .. 2 ounces.

and

Water.. 8 ounces.
Chloride of gold................... ....15 gr.
Chloride of ammonium.......................30 gr.

Pour the gold solution into the hypo solution, then add thirty grains of freshly prepared chloride of silver.

A very popular and pretty process is the Kallitype process, of which we give a formula below; we have printed on the paper, but never have made it ourselves. The printing is easily done, and the results pleasing, although to the writer's eye they have a dull, semi-sunken appearance, as if they needed a tonic.

THE KALLITYPE.

Coat stout but fine-grained paper with a solution of
Sodium ferric-oxalate ....6 drams.
Water...................................... ....2½ ounces.

Dry quickly without the application of heat, and print till the deeper shadow portions of the picture become visible. On removal of the print from the frame immerse into a 1½ per cent. solution of nitrate of silver acidified slightly with citric acid, when the picture will develop brilliantly and with all detail.

Finally wash in pure water. A yellow tinge may be washed away with a five per cent. solution of oxalic acid.

118

Printing

Blue paper can be toned; and brown and a particularly faded, uneven black tone can be obtained if one think it worth the trouble; we do not.

A pleasing adaptation of the blue print process is made with very little trouble; it is to sensitize albumen paper on the glossy side, print and wash as usual. The finished prints have more detail than in blue print and a gloss from the albumen that is grateful to certain tastes.

ENCAUSTIC PASTE, 1.

White wax..... ....1 ounce.
Spirits of turpentine............................1 ounce.

ENCAUSTIC PASTE, 2.

Pure wax ....500 parts.
Gum elemi..................... .... 10 parts.
Benzole..200 parts.
Essence of lavender............................300 parts.
Oil of spike.................................... 15 parts.

Finally we submit Newton's method of hypo-elimination by salts of lead, either the acetate or the nitrate of lead. "Make," he says, "a stock solution of the salts of lead before-mentioned, by dissolving two ounces" (of either) "in sixteen ounces of water. If nitrate of lead be used, the water would better be hot, as it dissolves very slowly in cold water. When the prints are fixed, wash them off in two or three changes of water, and place them in water containing two ounces of stock solution to every four quarts of water; they need remain in the lead water only from five to ten minutes, and then they should again be washed in a few changes of water, and the work is completed, and by applying the most delicate tests no trace of hypo will be found. When the lead solution is put into the water to receive the prints there will be produced a trace of carbonate of lead, which will give the water a milky appearance. If the prints are put into it in this condition, the albumen surface will be injured by the carbonate adhering to it. The carbonate should therefore be dissolved before the prints are put into it, which is done by adding a little acetic acid, just sufficient to make the water clear.

CHAPTER VI.

PRINTING BY DEVELOPMENT; HOW WE CONQUERED
THE BRILLIANT BROMIDE, AND HOW THE PEACEFUL
PLATINOTYPE CONQUERED US.

THE first bromide that we ever saw was one of our
own making. It was pretty poor. The shadows were
clogged, and the sky had a thunder storm not down on
the negative; and the edges were yellowed, and several
distinct black thumb seals showed where the enthusiastic but heedless operator (that was I; Jane is seldom
enthusiastic and never heedless) had shifted the position
of the paper in the tray.

The bromide process reminds me of the heroine in the
"Bab Ballads" who was "far from plain." So is it, very
far!

Our first developments were made on Eastman paper,
following exactly the Eastman formula.

It is a capital formula. It is a capital paper. The
only trouble was that we were not capital operators, a
third requisite in the case of bromides. The bromide is
reticent to excess. It never gives the very smallest
sign, misuse it in the printing frame as you may.

Snowy white it goes into the frame, snowy white it comes out.

At first we used to put our paper in on the wrong side; but we soon knew better than that. The curly side is the right side.

But to find the proper exposure was not so simple.

The formula says: "The exposure varies with the intensity of the negative and the quality and intensity of the light, but may be approximately stated to be, using as thin a glass negative or film as will make a good print, one second by diffused daylight, or ten seconds at a distance of one foot from a number two kerosene burner." You will perceive that the maker of that formula may well have been, in a previous "karma," a hired man of the Delphic oracle, accustomed to make a good weatherproof job, with plenty of room, inside, to turn round.

"The intensity of the negative varies—infinitely!" said one of the firm, "and light is about as bad; and how thin do you suppose a glass negative *ought* to be to make a good print?"

Jane had not the least idea; she supposed that we must find out by trying.

We did. Indefinite as that formula seemed to us, we do not see, now, how it could be more precise. Bromides are as indefinite as the average conscience. But there is this to be said for them; they are not fickle.

Printing by Development

They do not act like an angel with a certain exposure and a certain developer, one day; and turn into a vixen under the same circumstances, the next, which some papers do! It may be hard to hit on what they need to do their best, but once the proper environment *is* found, the print will work in it as evenly as parallel lines.

Discouraged by the apparent uncertainty of the oxalate process and the apparent complexity of the developer (which we had never tried), we developed our first bromides with our old friend, hydroquinone. But in our immeasurable innocence we exposed the prints according to the oxalate formula. Naturally, we came to grief; in fact, we came to nothingness, for the pictures did not favor us with a glimpse of themselves. By steadily increasing the exposure, we did arrive at the point of precipitation of the image at last. But we were not so much better off after we had captured the image, for all the whites turned yellow. This we judged to be due to over-strong developer and under-exposure. But we never did succeed in getting absolutely pure whites with hydroquinone. We told each other that a slight mellowness of tone was desirable and artistic. And we returned to the iron.

To obtain accurate exposures, we expose small slips of paper on the negative at different distances and for different periods, before a large kerosene lamp. We expose until we get an exposure and a lighting that will give clear shadows, full detail, and a desirable tone. Then we describe the exposure on the negative envelope; and that negative's future, in bromide, is safe. For instance, here is the thinnest of thin negatives, called "At Sunset." Beneath the title is written : "Good only in bromide, two seconds, two feet from copper lamp. Developer, oxalic acid, gray tones formula." The latter part of the description refers to another experience. We soon perceived that the developer could no more be constant than the exposure, and having fitted a developer to a negative we think it wise to label the pattern.

Almost our first discovery about bromides was that the color varies. The iron developer gives a different colored black from a hydroquinone or a pyro or an eikonogen. Moreover, the iron developer itself gives different tints. One print would have a clean bluish-black, velvety rich and soft; a second would show a distinctly olive dye in its black, like the doors of modern colonial houses; another, still, would be brown and not black at all; while a fourth would be all in the loveliest silver grays, deepening into a blue-black in the depths of shadow; and besides these standard hues, there were several mealy "sports," as gardeners call them. They all seemed to come at their own sweet will, independent of our wishes.

But one day Burton (who has always offered us a plank when we have stuck fast in the mire—we call it

IN OVERFLOW TIME.

being "mired up" in Arkansas) explained the brown tints. They were to be expected where negatives were exposed for an abnormally long time and development had been proportionately retarded. Having read Burton, the member of the firm who always "dares to put it to the touch, and win or lose it all," went into the studio and remained there an entire afternoon.

When Madonna came out to see how she was faring, the sun was declining, the cook was beating waffles for supper, the other maid was bustling to and fro through the passage, setting the table, the man was building the evening fires, and both the dresser and the whole of one table were covered with washing-boxes.

Blessings on the negro race! A white cook might have slyly scowled at the intruders from the studio, that took up so much space at the busiest hour of the day; but our black Jinny flashed her teeth at them, in liveliest sympathy. "Miss —— in dark room," says Jinny, grinning; "she ben doin' of dem little tricks de plum evenin'."

"Where are the prints?" says Madonna, fishing among the dismembered bits of pictures.

"*These* are my jewels," returns the photographer, emerging from the room with a neat combination air of Cornelia with the reporters and Horatius at the bridge. "This, lady, has been an afternoon of scientific exploration, not ornamental printing."

An Adventure in Photography

"I hope you haven't used up all the paper in your experiments," Jane puts in, advancing, and eying the bits in the water.

The scientist's life is ever a lonely one; he dwells on the heights, where there is rest but not much general society. But from that afternoon's derided experiments we really did learn the secret of bromide colors. The sepia tints can be produced at will, if one will take a strong negative, give it a long exposure and retarded developer. The green tones come under much the same causes, over-exposure and development kept back by bromide.

Whether, when one has gotten the brown and green tints, they are worth keeping, is another question. The brown tints, I may say further, will only come on well-balanced, dense negatives: but the green ones are more democratic and come on thin negatives, dense negatives, and medium negatives; but I imagine preferably on the moderately thin negatives.

The brown tone is brown and not a brownish-black, but it is a cold rather than a warm sepia. Bromide prints may be toned a warmer and evener hue without the minute painstaking that is necessary to develop them brown.*

Iron is the density-giving element, and oxalate the

* We append the formula. I only tried it twice, but obtained tones from red to brown easily.

detail giver in the iron developer. We have come to
developing our bromides tentatively, just as we develop
our negatives. We soak the print in most cases in a
tray of plain water for a few seconds or a minute. This
is only to soften the film. Where for any reason we
would not weaken the developer by even that minute portion of water that is left in the film, we soak the paper
in oxalate of potash solution. Then we rock the tray.
In a very short time, hardly more than a minute, usually,
the details begin to appear. We now add a little of
the iron solution to the oxalate. To make this addition
we ought to pour the oxalate into a graduate, and stir
in the iron with a glass rod, for there is great danger of
the developer not mixing evenly and the print developing
in patches, if the iron is simply poured into the tray.

I say we ought: we do as we ought about once
in thirty-five times. We trust to a little sleight-of-
hand that is the property of all trades, and blindly
trusted by all artisans of experience. We give two or
three rocks and expect to mingle the ingredients. We
keep on adding the iron until the print has nearly
enough density. Obstinate shadows we paint just as
we paint them in negatives, sometimes with concentrated developer, sometimes with iron, sometimes with
oxalate. Immediately before the development is complete, on the very edge of the last moment of grace,
there passes over the print an indescribable, flashing

change, every line sharpens, every tint deepens, it assumes that indefinable attribute that we call brilliancy. Now is the *crisis!* A second before this the print was flat, a second later it may become morosely dark; the developer must be poured off instantly and the paper be flooded with dilute acid to stop the development. Now the print is safe; it will not change again. You may not wash out the acid, or you may not fix sufficiently, or you may not wash enough at the end, and your picture, because of any one of these errors, may fade and perish, but so far as its present appearance goes it is out of danger. We sometimes prefer to finish our development in a tray of water instead of the acid, especially if we desire a soft effect. Water always has a softening touch. Generally we wash off the print in three baths of the acid water, and put it to soak in a tray of water to wait until the others shall be ready to accompany it to the hypo. We develop one print at a time, but we fix and wash a dozen or two in company. We like to fix them in two baths—a strong bath and a fresh weak bath. We make up the hypo afresh each time of using.

We have obtained good results by adapting the East-man formula to the tentative method of development thus described; and we have obtained equally good results by following the respected formulæ that you may see in the usual place, at the end of the chapter. We have

enamelled bromides in a simple way, by damping them
and squeegeeing them to an ebonite sheet. The squeegee
started in the world as a sink utensil, but it did its work
none the less effectively for its humble origin. They
are laid on the ebonite (or on a ferrotype) gelatine side
downward, squeegeed free of air bells, dried and peeled
off. That is the whole operation; and if the gelatine
coating is of normal thickness it is certain to be success-
ful.*

Bromide development is infinitely elastic, flexible, and
—best quality of all in man, beast, or bromide—*trusty.*
The rough papers can give something nearer to an
engraving effect than any other photographic paper.
They are richer and more translucent in their shadows
than the platinotype, their next friend and rival, or the
kallitypes. They may be printed independent of
weather or time, by night as well as by day, and they
are so rapid in their printing manual that they appeal
irresistibly to busy people. The more we know them
the better we like them.

In some respects, however, the bromide cannot come
near the proud position of another developing paper,
the platinotype. The balance of the scales is adjusted
by corresponding weaknesses; and if anything we prefer

---

* Cyanotypes (blue prints) can be treated in the same way. We
have obtained a high gloss on them, which seems (three years later)
to be lasting.

the bromides. When the question has to do with their faults, we can only say about both papers what Alice said about the carpenter and the walrus, " Well, they are *both* very disagreeable!" The bromide needs a strong and intrepid spirit to control its frantic pace; the platinotype requires the sleepless caution of Louis XI. or a sitting hen!

The virtues of the platinotype (of which you will hear in all the circulars) are: First, its simplicity. Excepting only Pizeghelli's modification,* it is the simplest of all photographic printing papers. Secondly, its independence of that contaminating Mephistopheles, hypo. The platinotype needs no fixing in hypo; it washes and cleans itself in easily managed baths of muriatic acid; and because it has no dealings with hypo, the final washing only takes half an hour, and is done by shifting from one tray to another in the most convenient way in the world. Thirdly, its flexibility; it stays where it is put, and always knows its place. These are virtues wherein it excels the bromide; other virtues that it shares with the bromide are its delicacy, its exceeding beauty, and its permanence. The faults of the platinotype (which you will find out for yourself) are its incurable, morbid sensitiveness to damp, and its uncertain printing.

The image should faintly show, one is told, but some

* And blue prints.

negatives need to show more than others. Print to precisely the depth that you have printed before, with happy success, and you may be horrified to behold your picture black and hard. The platinotype, also, asks a good deal of its original glass; it has nothing like the generous hospitality of the bromide to all sorts and conditions of negatives; no, its majesty must have a fine, dense, and vigorous negative, almost too hard for albumen printing. We prefer to make negatives especially for our platinotypes. The new cold process, however, is much more adaptable than the old hot process, and we have made good prints from decidedly thin negatives. But the printing scarecrow did not daunt us; we contrived to judge of exposures, although we should much prefer there were no image at all, since it comes but to betray; neither did its exclusive tastes in negatives drive us away; we have plenty of good, firm negatives; and if we have not we hope to make them in future—we are going to do considerable, like all amateurs, in that vague and omnipotent time. The black drop in the platinotype cup that makes us set it down untasted is none of these; it is that either we are not dry enough for the platinotype, or the platinotype is too dry for us! We did not once get really fresh paper; only once or twice did we get paper that gave us a hint of what fresh paper could do.

In fine, we were conquered. But we are hoping to

sensitize our own paper, obtaining the sensitizing fluids from Willis and Clements, the platinotype proprietors; and we anticipate, after the usual stumbles, that we shall be as fortunate as in our sensitizing of blue paper. We used the formula on the papers and found no improvements. We could get better prints when we printed in the bright sunlight than in the shade. And we fancied that we got sharper prints when the development was rapid than when it was slow; but that the slow prints were more delicate.

Rapid paper we tried, and have no reason either to detail our destruction of one box of aged paper that its inventor sold to the dealer as a first effort, and the dealer for years must have been trying to sell to some one else, or to point with pride to anything about the business.

The Pizzighelli paper is a black and white paper, very simple—a photographic babe could manage the process—and resembling a rather ineffectual and timid platinotype in its looks. It is developed like a blue print, but not printed so deeply. A few trials will indicate the necessary exposure.

Far more intricate, but to our taste far more fascinating, is the printing on positive films of celluloid. They take an infinitesimal exposure, a second by a faint lamplight for a thin negative has sufficed me, and needed the full dose of bromide in the developer to the bargain.

132

Printing by Development

— —

They make a beautiful, porcelain-like picture. Dense, brilliant negatives are best for subjects with them. It would please me to be able to remark something about lantern slides; but I can only say that in the language of Dr. Young, "Procrastination is the thief of time," and that is why we never arrived at the point of making lantern slides. Neither did we ever attack the most exquisite of all the photographic processes, the carbon process.

FORMULÆ.

Besides all the standard developers there are fancy messings wherein the uninitiated can discern no end nor aim except a determination to use as many drugs as possible. Hydroquinone and eikonogen all have admirers, and now comes a potent developer to which all the others are as infants. Dr. Stolze, who applied this agent to the development of bromide paper, adopted the formulas of Dr. Anderson, viz.:

(1)—Water ....32 ounces.
    Hydrochlorate of para-amidophenol.......85 grains.
    Sodium sulphite. ....1 oz. 5 dr.
    Potassium carbonate.....................6½ drams.

and

(2)—In boiling water .... 3½ ounces,

dissolve

Potassium metabisulphite................1 ounce,

and

Hydrochlorate of para-amidophenol.......3 drams,

and add to the solution, by constantly agitating it, saturated solution of caustic soda, till the precipitation formed is redissolved. The solution is used diluted with from 5 to 50 volumes of water, as exigencies may require.

An Adventure in Photography

A Developer that works well with All Kinds of Negatives, and Notes wherein is condensed the Wisdom of Portman, Grundlach, Adee, Janeway, and Others of the Wise.

A.—1 pound neutral oxalate of potash. Dissolve potash in the hot water. When cold (and be particular that it is cold, not tepid!) add 100 grains oxalic acid dissolved in 1 fluid ounce of hot water and cooled. Add half the acid solution at once, and the rest slowly, testing with litmus paper until bright red specks can be seen on the paper.

B.—Take 8 ounce bottle well cleaned and put into it
   960 grains protosulphate of iron (2 ounces Troy),
   100 grains citric acid,
   80 grains bromide of potassium.

Add distilled water (if you can get it ; we never could!) to make up to eight ounces. Shake well, and lay the vial on its side in a warm place until the crystals of iron are dissolved. This will soon occur, and the bottle will be full of a pale green, beautifully clear liquid which will keep well. We found it wise on account of the perishable and changeable nature of the iron to buy ounce bottles of powdered iron. These being kept away from the air kept very well. Another way is to fill up the sulphate of iron bottles with water, and whenever any crystals are taken out to fill up again with water.

To obtain gray prints take two drams of the iron solution to one fluid ounce of the oxalate. Give rather a short exposure.

To obtain dense black and white prints, add one half-ounce water to the gray mixture and give one or two seconds' longer exposure.

To obtain warm tones (so-called) take a perfect negative and about fifty per cent. longer exposure, adding three-fourths to one ounce of water to the oxalic solution.

This formula I copy from our note-book ; it is not ours, but Mr. A. A. Adee's. It is admirable, and has never once failed. Even our messings and variations of it have not affected its active usefulness.

Printing by Development

The clearing solution is a hundred grains of oxalic acid to one quart of water. We use about a gallon of clearing solution to a dozen 5 by 8 prints.

Eastman's fixing bath is a good one ; but one that pleases us especially is—

Fixing soda	200 grams (not grains).
Acid sulphite or double sulphite of soda	50 grams.
Water	1000 grams.

Alum is not needed with this bath.

NOTES.—It is well to have normal developer mixed in a graduate, and also some well restrained by bromide. We are not altogether settled in our minds as to the sphere and value of bromide. Undoubtedly it does all that its approvers promise in the way of restraint and contrast, but with us the question is, Does it impair the purity of the tones? Can you get as clean and rich a color where bromide is used in excess? Grundlach is positive that bromide is color safe. He uses bromide freely ; the more contrast needed, the more bromide. Sometimes he will have as much bromide in his developer as he has iron, and he uses sixteen times as much iron as Eastman's formula requests. He uses oxalic acid for clearing. One ounce to a pint of water for the first two clearings, half an ounce to the pint for the third clearing, and pure water for the fourth.

Imlah prefers long exposure and a weak developer to quick exposure and strong developer. Dense negatives need a developer weak in iron, and thin negatives as much iron as they can bear. In extreme cases he has used (and we know by experience that it is safe and profitable) as much as one to three for proportion.

Boracic acid makes a good restrainer in the stead of bromide. —(E. Audra.)

Never neutralize or acidify solutions by litmus paper at night :

An Adventure in Photography

lamp or gas light, being more or less yellow, gives uncertain values to color.—(Adee.)

The following toning bath answers well, after fixing, if the print is at all green :

Sulphocyanide of ammonium....................30 grains.
Chloride of gold................................. 1 grain.
Water... 4 ounces.

Half a minute in this bath will give the print a rich black tone ; a longer time will turn the print blue, which answers very well for moonlight effects."—(Portman.)

EIKONOGEN DEVELOPER FOR BROMIDE PRINTS (GEN. JOSEPH BROWN).

No. 1.

Sulphite soda (pure crystals)...................120 grains.
Water... 8 ounces.

Dissolve, and add
Eikonogen.................................... 60 grains.

No. 2.

Potass. carb. ....240 grains.
Water... 5 ounces.

Three ounces No. 1 to one ounce No. 2.

If made fresh, a few drops of bromide potass. solution may be added with advantage, but I prefer a developer that has been used already for negatives.

HYDROQUINONE DEVELOPER FOR BROMIDE PRINTS.

No. 1.

Sulphite soda (pure crystals)...................246 grains.
Water... 4 ounces.

Dissolve, and add
Hydroquinone .... 60 grains.

136

Printing by Development

No. 2.

Saturated solution carb. soda (washing soda).

Two drams No. 1 to one dram No. 2 ; add water to make four ounces.

These will develop successively a number of prints. The image appears very slowly, but soon attains full black tones.

No acid bath is required.

Transferrotype paper is a beautiful variety of bromide paper and quite as easily managed. To obtain warm tones on either it or the other brands, take, after fixing and *thorough* washing (this is most important),

Potassium ferricyanide	9 grains.
Uranium nitrate	8 grains.
Glacial acetic acid	5 drams.
Water	16 ounces.

Immerse the print in this toning solution. Tone to desired color, and wash in running water twenty-five minutes, or until print is free from yellow color. The toning solution is made by dissolving the ferricyanide (it will turn into ferrocyanide if exposed to the air, and be of no use; therefore care must be taken!) in the water, let it stand a few minutes, add the acetic acid and then the uranium. "The secret of success lies in washing the print free from iron and hypo before toning." I can testify to the truth of this.

CHAPTER VII

INTERIORS

GOOD interiors depend more on patience than on anything else. They are best taken on a very rapid plate. There is no rule that can be followed slavishly in their presentment. Everything is a question of lighting.

We began trustfully exposing by the rule, " As many minutes in-doors as seconds out-of-doors." And very queer pictures the rule gave us. I have taken an interior in two minutes, and I have prowled around a camera, to keep away intruders, for an hour and a half. It all depends on the amount of light your picture is allowed. The only way we could ever determine that fluctuating and deceptive factor in the making of a negative, was to expose small plates the time we thought nearly right, and add or reduce according to results. We were liberal in our dealings and commonly were rewarded by a good clear print. We use a small stop, for in interiors sharp definition is imperative.

There is a grave fault of negative plates that we often saw discussed in the books but never had experienced until we took a corner of a room, and beheld in the

138

A LIBRARY CORNER.

singular large circle of brighter light the blighting
touch of halation. How it came we never knew.
It never came again. Since that time we have encoun-
tered a multitude of articles in books and papers on
halation—what it is, why it comes, how to avoid it—
but we cannot lay our hands on our hearts and say that
we are one whit the wiser for this diffused light on the
subject. It was supposed that celluloid and other films
would be free from halation, which was laid to the
peculiar account of glass; but we have read that it
persists in films as well as glass. In spite of the noise
made, we are of the opinion that halation is very rare—
too rare for the average amateur, who has so many
nearer and more demoralizing perils to manage, to concern himself about it. It is, we venture to suggest to
the painstaking comrade, considerably easier to repeat
one negative in fifty or sixty or a hundred, than it is to
" back " all those fifty or sixty or hundred frightfully
susceptible dry plates with non-actinic backing.

A kind of second cousin to halation, which happens
frequently in interior view taking, is the glare on picture
glass. Usually it can be detected while focusing. Glass
can be deprived of this shine by coating it with a wash
of thin starch, or any other liquid substance that will
give a mat surface. We have found it even simpler,
however, to take down the picture and put something
else in its place.

An Adventure in Photography

The wise recommend lighting dark corners of the room to be taken, with lamps placed out of the angle of view. We have tried the scheme. We never could tell whether it did the least good or not. But it gives the photographer a sense of having done his duty, and that is gratifying.

Windows are the *bêtes noirs* of the interior photographer. They have a trick of becoming developed by the light until they are mere fuzzy white spaces, no vestige of window architecture, curtains, or space beyond being left. The best way of dealing with this dilemma, in our humble opinion, is to let them go on printing and take their own way; and afterwards, with a little alcohol and turpentine, or ferricyanide of potassium and hypo, and some camel's hair brushes, to reduce the window to a proper condition. One may, however, shut the blinds of the window and keep them shut until just before the time of completing the exposure, when the cap may be replaced and the blinds opened and the window exposed for the length of time sufficient to print it clearly.

I once took a pretty picture of a child asleep before the fire, his little curly head resting on the open leaves of a huge picture-book, the sunlight falling on him through two long windows on either side of the fireplace. It was a corner fireplace, and precautions had to be taken to avoid cross lights. He was taken asleep

---

because he could be kept quieter in that position. The
blinds of one window were closed, and opened later,
with the best result. The whole exposure did not take
two minutes, and the negative came up strong and clear,
yet soft, with a large range of half-tones. The pictures
on the walls, the carving of the mantelpiece, the pattern
of the Persian rug as well as the child's figure, on which
the picture was focused, all were beautifully defined.
Through the open space between the window curtains
one could see a dim lawn and trees. You could not ask
better windows or better light effects, and the child's
mother said, " Oh, doesn't he look sweet? It is *perfect*
of him!" Yet I never display that picture. It has a
trivial defect—trivial, but a bar to display; it is not
rectilinear, and the beautiful mantelpiece and the beautiful windows are too much like a hen-coop in outline!

Probably the swing-back was the culprit; the swing-
back is rather more "obsessed" than any of the other
evil-doers in the camera, and it is the peculiarity of its
mischief that it is in collusion with the ground glass;
and to look at the image on the screen one wouldn't
dream the lines were crooked. I dare say the explanation of the apparent rectilinear lines is that one looks
naturally only at the central plane in focusing. If any
careless amateur will hereafter glance at the top of his
screen and calculate whether he is making a coop out of

his walls, and thus be warned in time, my humiliation will not have been in vain.

Often, a fire is burning in the scene. It would be pleasant to include it. But when the negative has been developed the fire has vanished. This is because it has printed itself out of sight. A little painting with a reducing mixture will sometimes do wonders; but it is as well to help the reducer. A good plan is to take the picture with the fire unlighted but laid ready to light; then to cap the lens, light the fire, and give an instantaneous exposure with a large stop to the leaping flames. The changing from the small to the large stop will do no harm to the other parts of the picture, because the exposure is too short, but it will both increase the light on the lens for the instantaneous exposure and give a desirable, soft, broad effect to the image of the flames.

The most interesting interiors have some suggestion about them. But the ordinary amateur interior banishes suggestion as a crime. The room to be photographed is swept and garnished. The books on the table are placed in neat piles; no cheerful, homely litter is allowed inside the view angle; the pictures have the uncompromising severity of tidiness of the day after house-cleaning, in a New England mansion.

That interior of a fireplace would be improved if a large white cat—which I see at this moment purring in the sun—were blinking at its glow. But we did not

INTERIOR WITH FIREPLACE.

put the cat in, because a cat cannot be expected to blink in one position for half an hour! We have a cat that we shall put into a fireside scene some day, however— a cat certain not to stir, being a cat of cotton neatly printed into the breathing image of the creature.

We shall bunch the rug up about its base and put it into the position of its best perspective, and no one will ever suspect how meretricious is our art! We don't mind a bit being tawdry and theatrical if we can escape being found out.

Interiors need a small stop, as they require sharp definition. They are commonly taken with a very wide-angle lens; but such a lens must be managed with some caution, on account of its distortion. Who has not seen the giant chairs without legs and the unsupported tables looming up in the foreground of a picture of a drawing-room, which, to judge from the diminutive furniture against the wall, must be of immense size?

The flash light was hailed with a vast deal of enthusiasm as the Open Sesame to instantaneous photography in interiors; but this enthusiasm has cooled of late years. Most flash-light pictures have rampant contrast, a sorry slighting of detail, thick shadows, and a general chalky, undeveloped, half-baked look. There are amateurs that can make artistic flash-light pictures. We are not of these gifted souls. We do not affect the flash light. The babies of our families have not been

An Adventure in Photography

taken in their cunning little bathtubs and their sweet
little skins by their adoring aunts; not they, not by us!
They have been taken out-doors on their velvet lawns
under their noble trees, also under umbrellas; and we
think they look quite as pretty.

CHAPTER VIII

PORTRAITS ; A CONFESSION

" SAY, Miz—wud you all be willing to draw maw ? "
" Take your mother's picture? " says Jane. It is she
that is " Mrs. ——," and she it is that the slip of a girl
with the pretty face and bare little feet is addressing.

" Yes'm," answers the girl, nervously smoothing the
torn front of her calico frock ; " maw's pretty old, and we
caynt expect to keep her much longer. And sister and
me, we'd be right glad to come and holp you all's
black man weed the gyarden."

" Very well," says Jane with a quiet sigh ; " tell your
mother to come here some afternoon."

The mother appeared the next day, in her Sunday
attire, which was as unsuited to photography as to
fashion. She had a bright, figured gown, and a small
handkerchief pinned about her throat with a brass
breastpin.

She did not look to be much more than forty, and
said she was "right peart, ginerrally was nuthin' the
matter of *her*," when we politely inquired about her
health. I think that her daughter's solicitude was
simply her notion of the proper filial attitude.

10   145

An Adventure in Photography

We took her portrait, and the daughters honorably weeded the garden.

The experience is one often repeated, so often that it has become a sensible drain both on our purse and our time. At first we were so flattered that any one should want our pictures that we did not think of refusing the kind admirers. But admiration palls on the jaded taste ; and we would fain long since have lost our fame among our own people; but it will not wane, rather it increases, and the expense and the trouble thereof; and babies have been brought miles to our camera.

To do our sitters justice, they are perfectly willing to pay, and have been known to suggest eggs, onions, or chickens with sincere cordiality. We did, in fact, receive a fishing-rod (made out of the cane of the region) from a grateful mother ; and a grateful father was with difficulty dissuaded from sending us a live owl.

The southern planter is still the natural protector of his tenants, expected to supply all their wants, from brandy in sickness to photographs in health. If the " store " keeps oranges or lemons or apples, the desirer of fruit will buy them at any price asked ; if it has none, he will go cheerfully to the planter's house and get them for nothing ! But he will not be ungrateful—shades of tender frying chickens that never cost us a cent, and

HOW THE FOCUS BETRAYS.

Portraits ; a Confession

—

succulent young onions, so suited to our retired life, forbid the slander!

Myself, I am glad that I have been permitted to give so much pleasure with such prodigiously poor pictures as most of our portraits have been. I say most, I do not say all, because I see no reason why one should be a liar even to appear modest! Jane has taken some portraits of which any one might be proud; I have taken a few myself that would grade, according to cotton rating, as "good ordinary," if not "low middling."

The amateur who is expected to take portraits with a landscape lens must make up his mind that he will take bad ones. Two lenses ought to set the landscape photographer up in business; four to six, I am told, is none too many for a portrait studio.

It is not only the lens that waits to humble him. Portraits are a distinct art, to be acquired by long, patient study superadded to natural gift. The lighting, the posing, the focusing must all be learned afresh. Our first lesson was that, if we wished to do anything above mediocre work, we must keep out in the open air. When poor Sally S—— brought her baby four miles to have it "drawed," and we took the picture in the studio, by the open door, and only got about half a baby out on the plate, we became discouraged with in-door portraiture. Like Goethe, we cried for "Light, more light!"

147

An Adventure in Photography

But we soon discovered that light was not enough.

I took a portrait of Jane, out-doors. I rigged up a background of a dark green screen. I put the screen against the side of the house, making a wall about Jane, which I told her would give much the effect of top lighting from a skylight. She said that they always had reflectors in studios, so I reflected on her with a white tablecloth thrown over a side of the screen. It rather lessened the usefulness of the reflector that we had not thought to look after the sun, which had slipped round on the other side of the house and was lighting Jane obliquely through the walls of a comfortable Southern home. I persuaded Jane to wear a most becoming fur-trimmed jacket. She said it was not a summer jacket, and the day was warm; but I told her the temperature would not show in the picture and that she must be willing to endure a fleeting discomfort for the sake of art; so she put on the jacket, but she did not look as happy as those who love her would wish to see her look. I focused her very carefully, bearing in mind the precepts of a distinguished French photographer who focuses a trifle out of the sharpest plane, in order to avoid the necessity of retouching. Then I told her to assume a pleasant expression and look natural. I gave rather a short limit to the exposure, for the same reason that I had not focused sharply, namely, to soften the detail.

HOW WE BETRAY THE FOCUS.

Portraits ; a Confession

The plate was developed with pyro, as judiciously as I was able to develop.

The negative had plenty of contrast, but was lacking in half-tones. I said so to Jane. She replied very justly : " Come to think of it, there were no half-tones to take except in the face."

It was true. Jane's black hair and dark brown jacket were almost merged into the dark green background of the screen. This not only had a gloomy effect, it flattened the picture ; there was no relief, such as a light figure on a dark background will show. If I had taken the pearl-gray background which we always use now (formerly the waterproof covering of the piano), Jane's dark hair would have been outlined against it ; as it was, her hair melted into the screen, which was in admirable focus and told every one that it was made of green felt. Nevertheless I liked the picture and took it home with me ; and some one who knows Jane picked it up and said : " What a sweet, pale, sad face ! Who—why, it is Mrs. ——, isn't it ? But how ill she looks ! "

Now, Jane was in perfect health and in very good spirits at the time : but she certainly did look like a convalescent sitting up for the first time after a long illness.

And the reason was the dull lighting and the dark screen.

We never used the screen again. But it could have been used to good advantage with a different subject.

149

An Adventure in Photography

Instead of the green screen we used the pearl-gray travelling cloak of the piano, or a gray horse blanket. We moved our background well back to put it out of focus. This gives depth to the background and also softness. We try to get on the right side of the sun and use a sheet and a clothes-horse for reflectors. The sun, striking the reflectors, lights the side of the face opposite.

An alarming feature of the landscape lens is its short focus, which makes such uncomfortable contrasts between people's hands, held out a little way before them, and their faces. I can illustrate better by the full-length picture of the little boy and girl and the vignette than by description.

We had this difficulty, among others, to fight in the picture of Jane's Sunday-school class on the plantation, which is here given. If they were not on one plane they would be pygmies and giants; if they were on one plane they would be unendurably stiff. We did the best we could with the problem by putting the little children to the fore. Another difficulty was even worse; the mothers would expect as near a front face for each child as could be put into a picture; and that would be a wounded spirit whose child turned a profile away, while the mother of a child who turned his back on the camera would never get over it while life remained. And they were obliged to look at the sun, yet if they looked at the sun they would squint and blink! Jane,

THE SUNDAY-SCHOOL CLASS.

as usual, compromised with the irresistible. She arranged the children. The mothers said it was "a mighty pretty picture, and it favored" Tom, Dick, or Harry, "but it did look queer to see the children looking down that way; it would be a heap prettier if they were looking up," and Tom, Dick, or Harry had "right *nice* eyes!"

"Well," Jane said, as I brought her the first print, "it does not look like the stereotyped portrait group; but it does look as if it had worked awfully hard not to look like it!"

Foliage is the favorite background of the amateur, I suppose because he could not well find one more difficult to manage artistically.

The leaves are likely either to be a mere mussy blur or to be so insistent in their definition that they distract attention from the figure.

It is supposed that the dark greenery will give a background that will make the faces better lighted. Faces, the amateur soon finds, are dark in out-of-door pictures. But they need not be dark. If he relieve them against an azure sky they cannot very well be anything else, but if he will take the afternoon light and a side sun, with a rock, a tree trunk, or the grass for his background, he will have no trouble with his complexions.

Why is grass neglected as a background? for a child's figure especially it is admirable. It is not busy and uncertain, like foliage; its lovely half-tints and broad treatment (when properly focused, which means when not focused sharply or stopped down) have a restful softness; it demands nothing from the eye.

An umbrella is a pretty background for two little heads. But do not risk an instantaneous shutter on an umbrella except with powerful sunlight. You may bring out all the details of your picture; but again you may not; and if you have not plenty of time and plenty of plates and plenty of patience, it is not advised to risk the chance.

We do not say that foliage may not be used most effectively. Hundreds of examples would arise to confute such a rash critic as the maker of that assertion. We merely confess that leafage has frequently (in our persons) betrayed the heart that trusted it.

The frontispiece, however, shows Jane's latest portrait, where she uses a tree for background and has successfully overcome the difficulties.

It was taken late in the afternoon, on an orthochromatic plate; and, our own studio not being just then in order, it was developed very delicately by Mr. Hostletter of Davenport. The composition of this simple picture took over an hour. Indeed, we have spent a whole afternoon, more than once, composing a picture which we decided was not worth the taking; and have gone home without a mark on our plates.

HARRY.

Portraits ; a Confession

The larger stops are better for portraits, since they give truer values. In a portrait the figure is the impressive part, the rest should be subordinate.

We soon found that, with a wide-angle landscape lens, small figures were more satisfactory than larger ones. Unluckily, the mothers of our dear children—there are three mothers to the five children; and sometimes we feel that the proportion of mothers to be pleased to children to be pictured is too great!—all crave to have their children as nearly life-size on the cards as a five-by-eight lens can manage. This has led to rash experiments. And to disappointment. The usual result of portraits taken by a landscape lens is disappointment; and our first advice to an amateur intending to take portraits is, "Don't try to make furniture with a hatchet!" Buy a portrait lens, or keep your figures within the limits of the best work of your lens.

But the lens is the simplest, the nearest, step. Beyond is an illimitable vista of knowledge to be acquired. There is the whole art of composition. It is artlessly taught by some of the professionals, who divide pictures into classes, in the saw-and-hammer carpenter spirit. There is angular composition, and there is pyramidical composition, and circular composition, in the same manner as, in chiaro-oscuro, there are the technical divisions, light, half-light, middle tint, half-dark, and dark; and the honest man believes his duty done if he can get his composition into one of the classes and decide which lighting he will take. Generally he lights his sitters very much the same way. One man will recommend putting the lighted side of the face against the dark background, another the shadow, and it is only the rare man who sees that the face must decide.

The contour of the features, particularly the nose, is completely changed by lighting. In a three-quarter view, as the photographers call it, if the broad side of the face be in shadow the nose is straighter than if the shadow fall on the smaller side. The same face, also, will seem broader with the smaller side shaded than with the larger side partially in shadow. A professional photographer in a country town said frankly, " Well, I ain't got much use for these *artists*. They talk and talk, and they show pictures lit up splendidly, and mighty handsome just as pictures; but they don't please the sitters. And easy to see why! What folks want in photographs is to look just like themselves, only a heap better looking! And these artistic photographs make them look a heap worse. When a feller comes in to get a picture took for his girl, he ain't going to like it if his nose is crooked to make a striking lighting! 'Tain't in nature he should, neither!"

The photographer is between the two fires, his imperious art ideals and his more imperious sitters who want pretty pictures. I confess a sneaking sympathy with

THE GREAT SOUTHERN PROBLEM,

(Size of figure for landscape lens.)

the sitters. Have I not seen impressionist portraits of
beautiful children, that struck me as about the ugliest
caricatures ever sold for a great price? At the same
time the average " retouched " photograph, with its inane
smoothness and artificial youthfulness, would strike us
as ghastly did we not see it so often that our sensibilities
are blunted. A middle-aged woman, in a photograph by
the photographer intent only on pleasing, looks like herself painted to disguise her wrinkles. The photograph
gives a positively painful impression, akin to the impression my worthy friend would give were she to appear
enamelled and powdered and dyed into a fictitious girl-
hood.

I asked a professional photographer of my acquaintance, a young man with artistic ideals, a hard student
and an enthusiastic worker, how he contrived to please
his sitters and to satisfy his artistic conscience?

"I *don't*," he answered; "I do what the sitters want,
and then make the best job I can out of it.

" But," he added, thoughtfully, " I believe a sitter has
a right to be taken at his best; the trouble is, he usually
doesn't know what will give the best of him, and what
he insists on in position or lighting is more likely than
not to play the very mischief."

The best works for the amateur within our knowledge
are Robinson's " Pictorial Effect in Photography " and
" Wilson's Photographics."

An Adventure in Photography

They are likely to reveal such immeasurable possibilities that he will be warned in time.

If he shall not be, he can have no trustier guides.

It may seem both presumptuous and superfluous to offer our little dribble of knowledge obtained by experience, at the same time that we direct him to these fountain-heads; but from just these minute streams there is forming a river of practical knowledge for the amateur.

A few little points have come to us in portraiture, not novel, but useful. They are submitted with humility.

Stout people take better (that is, thinner) pictures standing, a standing position making their necks longer; for the same reason a thin subject should be seated.

When taking the whole figure, a three-quarters view gives better results than a full view.

The hands are almost as full of character as the face, and should be as carefully treated.

Unless the amateur have a studio with a skylight, it is of advantage for him to take his subject out-doors.

Orthochromatic plates are much the best plates for portraits.

Unless he have a portrait lens, a teachable spirit, some previous knowledge of art, and exceeding pa-

Portraits ; a Confession

—

tience, it is better for him not to attempt portraiture
at all.

That is our confession.*

* I have said nothing about retouching. It is a branch by itself.
If the amateur have, as one of us has, a smattering of knowledge of
figure drawing, he will find retouching a simple matter, especially on
unvarnished films. For a retouching medium, a little gum camphor
dissolved in Venice turpentine (the proportions are not of vital
importance, they regulate themselves ; when the mixture is thin
enough to rub on easily it will be right) will do all that one can ask.
And both landscapes and portraits can be helped by judicious, *slight*
retouching. Excessive retouching is baneful anywhere and always.
Any retouching is a confession of failure.

A few pencils, some Gihon's opaque, some neutral tint and Chinese
white, with a magnifying handglass such as most people have in the
house to inspect photographs, are all the necessary paraphernalia for
slight retouching. And much retouching we hold to be a wrong to
the negative. So we do not so much as allude to a retouching desk;
because there is in the credulous spirit of the beginner in amateur
photography, a blind yearning to buy things ; and we could never
forgive ourselves were any word of ours to encourage this pernicious
craving,

CHAPTER IX

THERE is a current phrase—" with the merciless fidel-
ity of a photograph." It shows how much most people,
especially most writing people, know about a photograph. A photograph begins to lie the instant it can
stand on its legs—that is, its tripod's legs. The lens is
an unconscionable liar; its wide angle was given it to
lie. The negative lies, for even orthochromatic plates do
not give the exact truth in color values, and no plates,
of course, give the colors of nature. And when it gets
along in its career to the printing period, there are
almost no bounds to be placed to the falsehoods of the
photograph. You can "print in" pretty much anything
you like. One day we amused ourselves by introducing
snow-capped hills into our flat forests. Nothing could
be easier, supposing the photographer to be a dabbler
in art to the slightest degree. We cut out of paper the
outline of hills, pasted it on the glass side of the negative, moistened the paper, and with the finger rubbed
away the fibre at the base of the hills so that the tree-
tops and part of the sky should print through the opaque
surface of the paper, softened the outlines by the same

trick, and, lo! " With verdure clad the hills appear, delightful to the ravished sense ! "

If you have a figure that you like, in a landscape that you don't like, you can (unless the figure should be lighted from the opposite side, which may happen) print your figure into the landscape that you consider best for it. This is not easy, but with considerable practice it can be done so neatly that it shall deceive the very elect.

Whether it is worth doing is another question. We don't think it is.

The manner in which we do it, when we are so abandoned by our artistic guardian angel as to do it at all, is to first trace on thick writing paper laid over the figure negative the exact image of the figure itself.

We then cut out this image with exactest care and a sharp, sharp knife. (Don't try to mangle it with the scissors.) We have the sheet of paper large enough to cover the entire negative; thus, when the figure is cut out, there remains a mask of the landscape.

Now we take a landscape and dispose this blank paper figure in any position that we like. Having painted it black or red, or any non-actinic color, we paste it on the back of the landscape, and print the landscape itself in the usual way. There will come out of the printing frame a landscape wherein stands, or sits, a clear white figure. Now the second mask comes into requisition. The printed paper is laid against the film of the first landscape, and the blank white figure is fitted with extremest nicety to the figure in the landscape, while the second mask, having been painted like the first, is fixed firmly over the glass side of the negative. The only thing that can print is the central figure, which prints accordingly. It is about a hundred to one that you will not cut the printed-in figure-mask exactly, and that, in consequence, portions of ground or shrubbery or some one else's clothes will stick (like a weird coat of tar and feathers) to the outline of the figure, or that you will have sliced off too much of him, or her, with quite as undesirable results; but if you have not done either of these wrong things, and have not pasted him on crooked nor lighted him in such a way as to suggest that he has " another sun than ours," nor printed him too dark or too light, nor printed the landscape in any slightest respect differently from the figure—if you have, in short, made a perfect piece of work of it, the figure will look as if it belonged to the landscape. On the whole, taking everything into account, perhaps your pathway through life will be less beset with briers, and your moral nature will blossom and bourgeon in better shape, if you let combination-figure printing alone.

The commonest form of combination printing is the printing-in clouds. There are two ways of doing

this, both greatly prized by professional printers, both
villanously abused. One is to decorate the glass side
of the negative, that it may dissemble and pretend to be
filled with clouds; the other, to make a regular cloud
negative, and print in the sky. Of course, only the
latter belongs properly to combination printing. But
the amateur in search of " wrinkles " will forgive my
treating of both methods of giving a skyless negative
a sky, here.

Burton suggests yet a third method of improving the
sky, although it gives no clouds. It is simply to shade
the lower part of the sky more than the upper, thus
making the lower part print more slowly, which will
necessarily make it a diffused lighter tint than the
other, and give a cloudless but shaded sky, such as is

often seen. To do this, after the print is made, it is
laid under a glass, flat, on the place for printing, and a
book or some heavy object is placed on the glass, on
which (the book) is laid a sheet of cardboard. The
book conceals the landscape portion of the print, and
the cardboard shades the sky.

An Adventure in Photography

The cut above will explain ; it is copied from Burton's "Photographic Printing."

"A is the sheet of glass with the print under it ; B is the book, or similar object ; and C is the piece of cardboard. Of course, printing must be performed in diffused light. Care must be taken to allow C to project so far beyond the book that the front edge of the latter will not cause an abrupt mark on the print."

But we have had as good if not better results from printing the negative shaded by a thick cardboard in the position of the diagram. A is the shading cardboard, B is the negative in an ordinary printing frame, C C are supports to keep A in position. The reader will kindly excuse the geometric formality and meagreness of the diagram ; it is caused by the inability of the present illustrator to wrestle with the intricacies of perspective involved in a presentment in full of the shapes of the printing frame, the cardboard, and the supports.

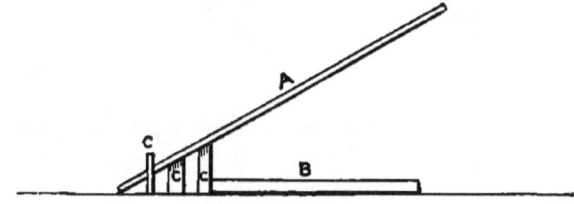

To return to the two cloud "stand-bys" of the profession. The decorator of the glass sometimes takes a burning match and smudges a little, sometimes he dabs

162

in a few cumuli with opaque, sometimes he pastes tissue paper over the original sky and with a crayon stub sketches any kind of sky that he wishes—or can sketch! Sometimes he considers the direction of the sun in the picture, more times he does not. And nothing is rarer than for him to consider the harmony between his sky and his picture; the consequence is that most professional skies have a labored air.

The commoner way, however, to get the sky into a picture, is to take a sky negative, or two or three, and to print them into every landscape that has no sky. The clouds are well developed and usually look thunderous. They make the picture look top-heavy. The subtle harmony between lighting, atmosphere, and sky is not given a thought; but it is not slighted for nothing; it always has its revenge.

We made some cloud negatives, and we printed them into our pictures without particular technical difficulty. We found that our easiest plan was to shade lower part of cloud negative, to print from it first, and to simply lay the print from the cloud negative over the landscape negative, and print into it. We took care to have our clouds high enough not to interfere too much with our tree-tops. We developed the clouds to make a thin, easily printed negative, and we used for the other a dense negative with a white sky; and there were no clouds visible out of the sky and plenty in the sky. Of

163

course, one can go to the trouble of masking his land-scape and of blocking out the landscape-tinted sky with Bates's varnish, but beyond the consciousness of having obeyed the doctors and the approval of his conscience, and very probably some white lines where the maskings have not quite fitted, he will gain little.

Technically speaking, our cloud printing was very decent; artistically, it rubbed our nerves the wrong way. Be as careful as we might about our lighting, consider as we might the character of our scene, read as we might, evening after evening, canons of art on skies, somehow our skies never seemed to belong to our land.

Two years ago we promised each other that we would give our entire attention to getting the very own original sky of each scene on to the plate, in the first place, and out on the negative, in the second; and eschew cloud printing-in and cloud negatives, forevermore.

We have never regretted that day. To our mind, the very best way to get clouds into the print is to take them there with the lens, and to fix them there with the developer, and to arrest them, should they flee, with the reducer.

It is too great a responsibility to invent a sky.

Vignetting can hardly be called a "trick" with jus-tice; it is not a deceiver any more than those kindly and wise people are deceivers who are silent about their neighbors' faults. The vignette tells the truth, but not the whole truth; and thereby often vastly improves the print.

Vignetting is one of the most charming photographic operations. Neither is it *very* difficult. It does not require a special "store vignetter," although one is convenient; vignettes for landscapes can be made of any size or shape, out of brown cardboard and tissue paper; and they will give as good soft vignetting as expensive glasses.

The very simplest form of vignetter is shown in the diagram below. A a is the printing frame, B b is the piece of stiff brown cardboard tacked tightly down on to the printing frame—for we do not want any stray interloping light coming in through the back yard—C c is the opening in the cardboard for the vignette.

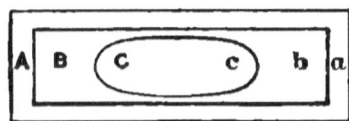

The higher the vignetter is lifted from the glass of the negative in the frame, the more gradual the vignette. A good way is to tack several thicknesses of cardboard on the printing frame, tack the vignette board on them, and paste black paper, such as comes with bromide and platinotype papers and is plentiful in every studio, over the board and frame, to exclude all light not invited.

Amateurs do not take the interest in vignetting that

the beauty of the results and the flexible and tractable nature of the process deserve.

They imagine that vignetting is an immense bother (which it is at first), and that it continues to be a bother to the end of the story (which it does not), and they will have none of it.

But vignetting soon becomes a simple operation. The vignetter, once adjusted to a frame, can be used, without the least attention, to make innumerable prints. And by using a larger printing frame than the negative, placing the negative in a carrier, vignettes can be printed (by the blue print and platinotype process of sensitizing) directly on cards, thus escaping all the annoyances of mounting.

The composite photograph is an amusing trick with a faint echo of scientific interest about it. We have unintentionally produced composites both of landscapes and people, but have never tried it in earnest. Neither did we ever attempt to depict a doppelgänger. According to the directions of Mr. Adee, it can be done (and he says easily done) by the use of an "opaque half screen, before or behind the lens, so arranged that two successive exposures can be made on the same plate, first on one half, then on the other."

Ghosts we have photographed. They are the easiest of all tricks. Your ghost is dressed in any spectral fashion you prefer; he is posed, and taken before some

solid article of furniture. Then he goes away, and a
trifle longer exposure is given to the scene, printing
firmly the furniture, which will show through the
ghostly figure. It requires no apparatus, and is taken
and developed like any picture.

I propose to put the mounting of photographs in this
chapter for two reasons. One is, that the whole prov-
ince of photography does not contain a process more
crammed with tricks, invariably of a malign nature,
than just this very mounting of prints; the other is,
that I have no other place in the book left for it.

Before a print is mounted you have to trim it. Perhaps you think that is easy. There is where we differ.
Perhaps you suppose that if you take a ruler and a lead
pencil and mark a line on a print, and cut that lead
pencil line with a scissors, you will cut your print
straight and true. Many educated and sensible persons, many noble and brave men, many sweet and
unselfish women, have thought the very same thing
before you; and they have said words that they ought
not to have said, and gone into tempers into which they
ought not to have gone, when they found out their
mistake.

You will seem to have cut a straight line; but unless
you have a very large pair of shears and smite the paper
in twain with one smite, there will be a tiny waviness
of line that your reason tells you will never be noticed;

but your eyes and everybody else's eyes will tell just the
contrary—after the line gets on the card. The only
sure way I know is to take a carpenter's square, lay the
print on glass, and cut with a sharp knife by the square,
or mark with a lead pencil by the square, and cut with
the shears. But if you take the shears, you may perish
by the shears, for a hair's-breadth of turning will show.
The knife is safe. Having trimmed the prints, you take
those that you have not ruined in successive trimmings,
and mount them. Albumen, bromide, and platinotype
prints are not all mounted in the same way, as we discovered when we wet the bromide print in which we
took pride, and laid it face downward on the glass.
There it remained, or at least the greater portion ; we
peeled *some* of the film off! Albumen and platinotype
prints, having a hard surface, may be wet and laid in a
pile on glass, or preferably on white oilcloth, smeared
one by one with the paste, and, as fast as smeared, placed
on the card ready for them.

It sounds so easy, doesn't it? In theory, the print is
placed in the centre of the card, and remains there to
be smoothed or rolled by the operator; and then it is
placed under a weight to dry. In actual fact the print,
though placed in the centre, slips somehow askew.
What it is aiming to do is to slip unperceived, so that it
may be pressed down, and the operator will be deceived
until he holds it up to look ; and then he will have to

soak it off with infinite labor, and it will go on wrong
again, and he will get "rattled," and the paper, because
of so much soaking and pulling about, will tear viciously,
and the end of these sorrows will be a ruined print! If
you mark the exact middle of your card and two dots
where the middle of your print must go, you will a little
decrease the risks of mounting.

After the print is safely placed in the middle of the
mount, it is either rolled with a convenient little roller,
which you can buy of the dealers, or it is smoothed with
a rag and the hand. The wee-est, most unobtrusive
grain of paste, that is not big enough to be called a
lump, is big enough to show and disturb the level of the
paper. The paste, unless very thin, rolls up in waves
and makes bubbles and mischief generally ; if very
thin it will not stick, and the corners will curl off the
paper.

But, usually, the roller will roll most of these annoyances away.

No roller, however, will make the cardboard dry at
the same pace as the print, and no weight will keep a
cockling paper straight after it has been taken off. We
put a small brickyard on top of some boards holding
down albumen prints, once, and the day after they came
out of the brickyard they were as lively as before, and
twisted themselves into concaves before twenty-four
hours were past.

An Adventure in Photography

I lay before the reader a number of mountants of great pretensions, with the hope that they will treat him better than they have us. The only stratagem that worked well in our hands was to wet both cards and prints equally wet—that is, soak them both. They then dry with something like an equal contraction. Bromide prints do not cockle like albumen, being only wet on the back, and platinotype prints are a pleasure to mount. So are blue prints.

The aristotype is the slipperiest dodger of them all.

It cannot be handled recklessly, for it tears more easily than the albumen—which is not necessary in order to be troublesome; it cannot be laid face downward on the glass, wet, lest it never come away; it must be dry on one side and be brushed with an alcohol mountant, which dries with frantic speed; so that wherever it is laid on the card, *there* it must stay! There is no second opportunity for the aristotype. However, we *have* soaked it off with warm water, and nothing in the shape of an awful warning has happened to us. The alcohol mountant is truly the discourager of hesitancy, but it has great virtues; among which stands high its comparative freedom from cockling. If it can have a dry print to mount, the cockling will be hardly perceptible; but no mountant can see a soaked albumen print through the press in safety, entirely unwarped.

170

Tricks

FORMULÆ.

To Keep Unmounted Albumen Prints Flat.

Soak them in equal parts of alcohol, glycerine, and water ; dry between blotting paper under slight pressure.

Solution for Mounting Prints Without their Cockling.

Nelson's No. 1 photographic gelatine	4 ounces.
Water	16 ounces.
Glycerine	1 ounce.
Alcohol	5 ounces.

Dissolve the gelatine in the water, then add the glycerine, and lastly the alcohol.

Permanent Paste.

Arrowroot	10 Gm.
Water	100 Gm.

in which 1 gram of gelatine has been soaked, and boil. After cooling add 10 grams of alcohol and a few drops of carbolic acid.

171

CHAPTER X

TO AMATEURS ONLY

WHETHER it come from the chastening influences of their art (which can be warranted to subdue a larger acreage of vanity to the individual than any other, unless it be literature in the early days of authorship, when the author is being introduced to the " readers " of the magazines), or whether it be due to the natural attraction of photography for choice spirits, amateur photographers, for the most part, are amiable, modest, and engaging people. They have none of the hysteric sensitiveness of the artist soul in the avowed arts—music, painting, or the drama, for instance. They do not spatter the pages of the photographic journals with spite, thinly masquerading as sarcasm ; rather, they exchange formulæ and " wrinkles " like brothers. They praise each other's pictures, and, outside of the " naturalistic " school, they do not feel themselves better than the rest of the world. They only feel themselves a little better than the kodak and hand-camera persons, who are, no doubt, very well in their way, but whose way is not theirs, as the all-wool coat said to the linsey-woolsey.

172

To Amateurs Only

It has been a pleasure to Jane and me, who have never felt that we knew enough to write to the photographic journals, to add our homely record of experiences to the multitude that will claim your attention, comrades of the camera.

I fear, however, that it is a little with me as it was with the unfortunate Irishman who was sent to dose the pony. He was given a bolus, and a tube through which he was to administer it. Presently he returned, very dejected.

"Well, Pat," says his mistress, "did you give the pony his medicine?"

"Shure, an' I did, me lady."

"Has it done him any good?"

"Sorra a bit, me lady."

"Why, Pat, how is that?"

"Well, me lady, it come this way. I put the stuff in the thing yez given me like yez towld me, and I put it in the crater's mouth, intinding to blow it down him, and I got all ready; but, bad cess to him, the baste *breathed first*, an' it wint down *me* instead of him!"

I have some compunctions lest most of the practical photographic medicine that I have collected will benefit only the collector. Nevertheless, I shall venture to add to it a very few precepts drawn from our own grapple with the powers of light—and darkness.

173

An Adventure in Photography

It is as true of the photographic world as of the universe, that which quaint old Jeremy said two centuries ago: " All parts of the scheme are eternally chasing each other like the parts of a fugue ! "

But one *motif* continually recurs ; it is the *motif* of beauty or of art (but what is art save the effort to realize beauty ?), and it persists through every stage in the making of a sun-picture. There are those who will have it that the instant the photographer slips the black slide before the invisible picture on the plate, the work of the artist is over ; the remainder is pure technique, clever artisanship, not art.

Comrades, don't believe them ! It does not ask the same kind of insight, or so high a gift of selection, to balance the negative properly in its development, to secure soft tones, and varied harmonies of chiaro-oscuro, and luminous perspective, as it does to compose a picture. Neither, I will admit, are the masters of style to be permitted to sit in the presence of the " makers," the poets and the seers ; but the master of style must needs be an artist, and a true one ! There was never, since the world began, a perfect artisan who had not some touch of the artist's soul within him. There was never a photographer who could bring out all the marvellous, delicate loveliness that the sun etches on a gelatine film, who had not the artist's intuition. He may not know a phrase of the gabble of the schools, he may not be able

174

to tell a copy from an "important" work, but the robe
of our Lady of joys and sorrows, will have brushed his
ignorant eyes all the same; unwittingly, perhaps, he
follows after her.

Nor can he part company with her in the further
mechanical processes of his craft. He needs must have
some help from her in his printing as well as his developing; although printing is vastly more mechanical
than developing. I don't think he need bother her to
stay through the mounting process, which is quite as
much a matter of paste as of eye, and as much a matter
of hand as of either, and in a better regulated world (say
Mr. Ingersoll's ideal sphere, where health is catching
instead of disease!) will undoubtedly be done entirely
by machinery.

Believing these things, comrades, and being ourselves
merely honest artisans (Jane insists on the plural pro-
noun, although, in candor, I think she gets an occasional
swish of the Lady's robes, herself!), we nevertheless
strive to be artists, just as good Christians strive to be
perfect, even though they are sure (except in the Meth-
odist Church) that they can't be!

And the practical rules of life that we follow are:

I. Before you go out with your camera, decide what
kind of a picture you will take. Determine rather to
take one view that will satisfy your conscience, than
eight or ten or whatever the number of plates you can

carry, that are hastily composed and by consequence poor.

II. Use a glass plate, and in most cases a slow plate, for landscape work. If you take animals other than the tranquil cow, you may require quick plates and the shutter. That will be your misfortune, not your fault.

III. Be infinitely careful about dust! This is technique, but so is the mixing of colors, and it counts as much. Wipe out your bellows with a damp cloth, and wipe your lens with a dry silk cloth. Keep your plates in your bag until you expose them, and your bag off the ground, for you must be as watchful of damp as of dust.

IV. In the field, plant your camera firmly. You cannot keep it firm on a windy day, neither can you use a slow plate, and your foliage will be "mussy" even with the shutter; therefore, never take photographs on a windy day. There is enough irritation and vexation and humiliation about the business without hunting all three in a pack!

V. Having composed as well as your natural limitations and ignorance will tolerate, focus according to the scene. If you wish to direct attention to one particular point and to gently obliterate or send to the dim background all other points, focus on the important object through a large stop. If you would have the eye explore the whole landscape, and wish nothing slighted, use the small stops. The smaller the stop, the deeper the focus as well as the sharper the definition.

VI. Do not focus through your largest diaphragm, and then put another stop in and expose the picture, without focusing again through the smaller stop. You may have reason to change the focus with the small stop.

There is a whole battlefield beyond this question of focusing. Dr. Emerson has said some of the most penetrating things about photography in its relation to art, that ever have been said; but there remains—without contravening the position of the naturalists—a fact which every amateur recognizes, namely, that it takes far more of an artist to compose an impressionist picture than a plain, downright, sharply focused one. Too much can hardly be said of the beauty of Dr. Emerson's own work; but Dr. Emerson's precepts followed by a beginner are likely to give sorry pictures of woolly ground, and foliage that appears to have been out ginning cotton !

VII. In removing or replacing the slides of your plate-holder, take your time. At least, take enough of your time to be deliberate and not to jar the camera. The slightest jar will show in the image.

VIII. Use orthochromatic plates.

IX. Try the tentative method of development. Be patient with your negatives. *Festina Lente!* An hour is well spent developing a really beautiful negative. Two or three negatives are enough to develop in one evening.

X. Decide what plate, what developer, what printing process will serve you best, and concentrate your efforts on that. The specialist has as great a field in photography as anywhere else.

XI. Buy all the photographic books and papers that you can afford, and read them. Make the acquaintance of professional photographers, and learn what you can from them. In many cases it is a good plan to have your printing (in any kind of paper which it is not convenient for you to manage) done for you by them. Business relations will facilitate the interchange of thought.

XII. Constantly, while you walk or ride or drive, study the scenery with an imaginary lens between you and it. Compose imaginary pictures out of the landscape. Notice the varied lighting. In fine, if you can't be an artist, be as much of an artist as you can.

And, whether you ever learn to draw real pictures with the sun or not, you surely will learn to behold new beauties in the familiar face that blesses us every day. Because you have learned the order of the shining of the sun in photographs, you will find yourself watching it in pictures, and from your study of the quality of scenery in nature you will recognize when a man shall

178

have told the truth about nature on canvas. You may not become an artist, but you will become a lover of art.

"I think what we have gained from photography is worth all the money and the trouble it has cost us," said I to Jane.

"It is worth more!" said Jane.

www.ingramcontent.com/pod-product-compliance
Lightning Source LLC
Chambersburg PA
CBHW020057030726
47498CB00006B/1836